Tracks
IN THE SNOW

Other Avon Camelot Books by
Lucy Jane Bledsoe

THE BIG BIKE RACE

Tracks
IN THE SNOW

LUCY JANE BLEDSOE

AN AVON CAMELOT BOOK

AVON BOOKS, INC.
1350 Avenue of the Americas
New York, New York 10019

Copyright © 1997 by Lucy Jane Bledsoe
Published by arrangement with Holiday House, Inc.
Library of Congress Catalog Card Number: 96-52915
ISBN: 0-380-73230-0
www.avonbooks.com

First Avon Camelot Printing: January 2000

CAMELOT TRADEMARK REG. U.S. PAT. OFF. AND IN OTHER COUNTRIES, MARCA REGISTRADA,
HECHO EN U.S.A.

Printed in the U.S.A.

OPM   10   9   8   7   6   5   4   3   2   1

For Marion, who loves animals and trees

Contents

1: A Hectic Friday Morning

No one believed Amy was missing.

Mom and Dad, busy getting ready for work, were angry about the weather, which was turning bad in time for the weekend. It was April, which meant it *should* have been spring. But we live in a small town in the Sierra mountains of California. Up here you can't count on spring until June. On this Friday morning, flat, grayish snow clouds hung over our world.

"Dad," I said, bringing him a second cup of coffee, "I think Amy's in trouble."

Dad was busy shaving, so all he did was mumble, "She'll show up. She probably just forgot."

There was no way that Amy would forget *me*. I told Dad, "I doubt that. There's got to be a good reason she didn't show up."

Mom pulled her nylons up one leg. She sighed and said, "It's so hard finding a reliable babysitter."

"Amy is very responsible," I told her, even though it wasn't completely true.

Mom said, "If Amy was responsible, she would have been here last night at six o'clock." She put on her light blue blazer and looked at herself in the mirror. Then she looked at me. "What happened to your glasses, Erin?"

I didn't have to answer. It was obvious. I had broken them. Again. When I jumped out of bed that morning, I'd landed right on them. At least only one leg broke off. I pulled the glasses' leg out of my back pocket and held it up for her to see.

Now Mom was *really* in a bad mood: the weather looked more like winter than spring; she and Dad hadn't gone to the movies last night because Amy never showed up; and now I had broken my glasses.

She sighed again but didn't say anything more about the glasses. "I'm late, Erin, but I don't want you wearing jeans to school and you know it. Don't forget to brush your hair, either."

"This is the first time Amy hasn't shown up!" I protested.

"Gotta run," Mom said. "No jeans and brush your hair."

Mom and Dad crashed into each other running for the door. Mom's coffee splashed onto her blazer.

"Go get the truck started," she told Dad, then ran back to their bedroom to change. A minute later she came out wearing a yellow sweater with a small glob of tomato sauce hardened onto the sleeve. I didn't tell her about it.

"Don't worry about Amy," she said running out the door.

I wanted to shout, "You don't know anything about Amy!" After watching the truck roar off, I sat down to eat my cereal.

I knew a whole lot about Amy, even though I'm ten and she's sixteen. We'd met last month when Mom and Dad hired her to babysit me during spring break. We spent two whole weeks together. She scared me that first day because of the way she looked. Mom called it the look of an artist. Amy has wild gray eyes that change all the time, like the mountain sky. She's real skinny and has long black curly hair. She always wears dangling earrings, which she makes herself, and about ten bracelets on each arm. They jingle every time she moves.

That first day, Mom said, "I would prefer that you two stayed home today. If you do need to go somewhere, call me first." Then she gave Amy her work number.

The minute Mom and Dad left for work, Amy said, "What are we going to do today?"

I shrugged.

"What's that cart out front?"

I was happy that she had noticed my covered wagon. I love reading about the pioneers who crossed the Sierra Nevada about a hundred and fifty years ago, looking for gold and fertile farmland. Unfortunately, I was born too late to be a pioneer.

But I'd always wanted to travel by covered wagon. So Dad and I built one. We started with an old red wagon. Then we cut some willow boughs, because they bend easily, and bought some white canvas. The hard part was attaching the curved willow boughs to the insides of the wagon, but Dad managed it by nailing them to some two-by-twos that fit tightly along the length of the wagon interior. Finally, we sewed the canvas into a cover that fit over the curved boughs. The wagon handle was the yoke for the oxen.

Mom helped me outfit my covered wagon with some old eating utensils, a length of cord, a pail, and a small shovel. I strapped the stuff to the outside, just like the pioneers did, and used an old blanket on the inside for my bed. It was a bit small, but I took naps in there anyway. To make it look authentic, Dad cut an extra square of canvas and sewed it on the covering to look like a patch. Once I tried to attach my cat, Snowball, to the wagon handle, but she wasn't about to pull anything. Dad said cats have much more dignity than oxen.

I explained all this to Amy and also showed her my collection of pioneer books.

"We have so much in common," she said, clapping her hands. Her bracelets jangled.

"We do?"

"Sure. I want to show you something. Come on. Let's take your covered wagon."

Before I knew it, we were locking up the back door and pulling the covered wagon out to the street. There were several feet of snow on the ground, but Mom had shoveled our walkway and the streets were plowed. Amy held the wagon handle and insisted I climb in. "I'm an ox," she said, laughing. She pulled me right out to the highway.

I was inside the wagon, so I couldn't see much, but every once in a while, I looked out. Amy pulled me right down the highway to where it intersected with the other highway. Now and then a car honked because, with all the snow lining the road, there wasn't much of a shoulder.

"Maybe you can meet my boyfriend later," she said.

I didn't say anything. Already we were breaking one of Mom's rules by leaving the house without calling her. I knew Mom and Dad didn't like my babysitters' having friends over, particularly boys.

"Want to?" she called out, now puffing from pulling my weight in the wagon.

"Okay," I said.

"He's taking me to the prom. It's at the end of May. I can't wait."

"What his name?"

"Justin."

"I bet you'll look real pretty at the prom."

"Thank you, Erin!" She stopped pulling and bent down to look in the opening of my covered wagon. "That's very sweet of you to say."

The sun struck her from behind, making the red highlights in her hair sparkle. I almost told her how pretty she was right then.

"We're almost there," she said.

"Where?"

"The place I want to show you."

This stretch of the highway was uphill and I suggested that I get out so that the wagon wouldn't be so hard to pull.

"Nope," she said. "I'm your ox, remember? I'm pulling you all the way to the top."

A few minutes later, breathing hard, she said, "Now you can get out."

We were at the intersection of the two highways. It was midmorning, and a Monday, so the only traffic was an occasional truck lumbering by. I climbed out of my covered wagon and pretended that I had come from Ohio, that I had traveled for six months to get here.

"Last summer," Amy said, "Justin showed me an old cabin out there." She waved her arm toward the timber-covered hills beyond the high-way. "A miner once lived there. One of your pioneers, Erin. I just may go live there one day."

"By yourself?" I asked.

"Oh, no! I'll have lots of company. There are squirrels, deer, and lots of coyotes."

I guess I looked a little unsure because Amy said, "You like dogs, don't you, Erin?" I nodded. "Coyotes are nothing but wild dogs. Remember, *all* living things are precious." Her face became very serious, her dark gray eyes like storm clouds.

"You know what?" I finally said. "I think you're right: we *do* have a lot in common. Because I love animals, too. I'm going to be a vet when I grow up. When we get back home, I'll show you all my pets."

"Good." Amy said, suddenly laughing. "You want to see *my* pets?"

I nodded.

She waved her arm out at the forest. "The trees are my pets. They give the best hugs of all. Come on, try it." Amy jumped into the snow on the side of the highway. The snow was fresh back then, so she sank into it up to her thighs. She pushed through it to one of the sugar pines, where she wrapped her arms around the trunk and hugged the tree.

"You're crazy," I said.

"I bet you are, too," she said, letting go of the tree. "Anyway, one day I'm going to live in that miner's cabin. All by myself. Except of course for the coyotes and trees. They'll be my friends. I'll drink from the streams and eat berries and roots for food. The birds will make my music. And I'll make a bed out of piles of dried, soft moss. What do you think?"

"You can't really live out there, you know," I told her.

She pushed back through the deep snow to where I waited with the wagon. "Why not?" she asked. "The pioneers did it, didn't they?"

"Well, yeah." I thought about that. "But they knew a lot. They were really prepared. It's not easy finding food or staying warm."

"Don't be so practical, Erin."

She looked kind of sad when she said that, so I stopped arguing with her. It didn't really matter that she didn't know how to be a pioneer. After all, she wasn't *really* going to go live in the woods.

"Tell you what," she said.

She didn't go on until I said, "What?"

"You can be my confidante, okay?"

I said, "Okay."

She laughed and said, "Do you know what a confidante is?"

I didn't want to admit that I didn't know, especially since I'd just said I'd be one, so I nodded.

Luckily, she explained anyway. "A confidante is a very, very important listener. You have to swear, though, that you won't tell a living soul about my miner's cabin." She held up her right hand.

I held up my right hand, too, but warned, "I'm not allowed to swear."

"Then promise on the threat of death."

I looked out toward the snowy hills and just then an icy breeze blew through. I shivered and said, "I promise I'll never tell anyone about the cabin."

"Good. Climb back in the covered wagon." Holding the wagon handle, she ran back down the hill fast, snorting and grunting, pretending she was a runaway ox.

Mom and Dad never learned that we had left the house that day. Nor did they learn about any of the other rules we broke during spring break. Maybe Amy was irresponsible. But I knew that she wouldn't forget to show up to babysit unless there was a good reason. We were friends.

By the time I finished my cereal, I was already late for school. I ran to my bedroom to change out of my jeans and—the animals!

Earlier that morning I'd let them out of their homes—except for my cat, Snowball, who's allowed to move freely around the house, and the fish, Lips and Fins, who can't leave their aquarium—and forgot to put them back. Dorothy, my guinea pig, was in a cubbyhole in my desk. She had pooped on my social studies report, which was due that day. I put her in her cage, then looked and looked for my two snakes, Scoot and Ooze, and finally found them curled up under my dresser. They went back to their terrarium. Quickly, I fed everyone.

Finally I shoved my homework, including the social studies report, à la guinea pig poop, into my knapsack and ran out the door.

2: Keeping My Promise

I RARELY WALK anywhere the direct way, even when I'm late. If there are cars around, it's hard to pretend to be a pioneer. So I often take a long-cut, the opposite of a shortcut.

That day I headed behind the buildings on Main Street so that I could walk in the woods. Usually I'd pretend to be someone like Sacajawea, who led Lewis and Clark west, or Calamity Jane, an outlaw in the Old West who was a skilled horsewoman and expert with a rifle. Today I noticed a set of deer tracks in the snow and followed them, pretending I was an Indian hunter and my whole tribe depended on me for food.

After a while, the deer tracks led deeper into the woods. I turned in the other direction, toward town, and began running to school.

I stopped when I saw the police station.

My watch said I was already five minutes late for school. Then I looked at the sky. The flat, grayish clouds were piling up into real storm clouds, puffy with dark gray bottoms. Even the air smelled like a storm: sharp and metallic.

The more I thought about it, the more convinced I became that Amy had run off to her miner's cabin. Just last weekend she had babysat me while my parents went to a birthday party for Dad's boss. Amy was really sad that night. For the longest time she wouldn't talk at all. Then, around nine o'clock, she started crying. I brought her a bowl of chocolate ice cream. I brought her Snowball to hold. I showed her the tricks Scoot and Ooze can do. Nothing would make her smile.

Finally I sat beside her and said, "What's wrong?"

She shook her head. She probably thought I was too young to understand, even though I'm ten. So I said, "Remember, I'm your confidante."

A tiny smile lifted the corners of her lips. She took my hand and said, "Yes, you are."

"That means you have to tell me what's wrong."

"Mama got a promotion. She gets a whole store of her own to manage."

"That sounds great."

"The store is in Tucson. And the job starts right away. We have to move within two weeks."

My first thoughts were selfish. I hated all babysitters except Amy. There was Mrs. Murphy, who was mean and strict. And Sonja, who talked on the phone the whole time she was here and completely ignored me. I blurted out, "Maybe you can come back and babysit me during the summer."

"Oh, Erin." Amy smiled again and squeezed my hand. "This means I'll have to start a new school when there are only a few weeks left. And we just moved here a year ago!"

Then I thought of something awful. "You won't be able to go to the prom with Justin!"

She let loose a fresh storm of tears. I tried to pet her long curly hair the way Dad pets my hair when I cry.

Her nose was all snotty and tears were still pouring out of her eyes when she said, "Justin never asked me to the prom."

"He *didn't?*"

She shook her head. "I made that up. Last month, when Mama first applied for the new job, I told her he asked me so that maybe she wouldn't make me go."

"Why did you tell *me* that he asked you?"

"I don't know. I guess I liked the idea. I got to pretend that he had. I got to pretend that Mama and I were going to stay here. I'm sorry I lied, Erin."

"That's okay," I whispered.

"But Mama *has* to take this new job. It's a promotion." Then she said, "It doesn't matter. Nothing matters."

"Lots of things matter," I said.

"Like what?"

"Mom and Dad. Lips and Fins. Snowball. Scoot and Ooze. Dorothy. My covered wagon. Um . . ." I knew those were my things. I tried to think of things that might matter to Amy.

"Sometimes I wish I could just disappear," she said.

"Don't say that." My voice came out in a whisper again.

"If I can't tell you, my confidante, who can I tell?"

Right then I felt more grown up than Amy. I reminded her, "Remember you said that all living things are precious? *You're* a living thing."

Amy's head lifted. Her gray eyes flashed as if there were tiny lightning bolts in them. "You're right," she declared. "You're absolutely right."

She seemed happy then and we watched TV until Mom and Dad came home an hour later.

Now, standing in front of the police station, I couldn't help thinking about what she'd said about wanting to disappear. What did she mean?

I got up my nerve and went into the police station. The line of people waiting to talk to the clerk at the counter was long. I didn't have time to wait. This was extremely important. Officer

Foster, who had spoken at my school earlier that year, was sitting at a desk, scowling at a huge stack of papers. I needed to talk to an officer. So while the clerk was helping someone else, I pushed right through the swinging door and marched over to Officer Foster.

Officer Foster looked up, still frowning. He had a thick brushy mustache and hairy ears. "Help you, young lady?"

I wondered what to tell him. I was sure that Amy had gone out to her miner's cabin. But I had promised not to tell anyone about that. How could I get the police to go find her without breaking my promise?

"I'm here to report a missing person," I said.

He smirked—just a little smile at the corner of his mouth. "And just who might be missing?"

"My babysitter, Amy Johnstone."

"And what makes you think Amy's missing?" When he spoke, his mustache hopped up and down.

"I have evidence," I said.

"And what might that evidence be?"

I didn't like his tone of voice and wished he didn't start every sentence with "and."

"She was supposed to babysit me last night. She never showed up."

"Well, now—"

I interrupted Officer Foster. "You don't know

Amy. She and I are special friends. She *definitely* would have shown up if she weren't in some kind of trouble. I know this for a fact."

Officer Foster leaned forward and looked at me hard. "And if Amy were missing, don't you think her mother would have reported it? We haven't had any calls of that kind."

"Her mom isn't home. We called a bunch of times."

"I'll tell you what," he finally said. "I'll send out a preliminary search. A little check around Sacramento, San Francisco, the cities, okay? Thank you for your help, young lady. You're a fine citizen."

He quit smirking, but I knew he was just playing along to get rid of me. He turned his back and started ruffling through papers again.

"But she may be nearby," I persisted. "You should do a search of the forests."

He glanced up, and for a second there was a little flicker of interest, like he might be taking me seriously. Then he leaned back and clasped his hands behind his head. "So you think you know how to handle this better than the police?"

"No, but—"

He looked at his watch. "Aren't you supposed to be in school, young lady?"

"Yes, but—"

"What's your name?"

I hesitated. "Erin Flaherty."

"Perhaps, Erin Flaherty, you should worry a little more about your own delinquency than about your babysitter's whereabouts."

That word "delinquency" made my ears flame hot. Suddenly the police station smelled like old coffee and car grease. I wanted to run out of there, but my feet were stuck to the floor.

Officer Foster rose and called to the clerk. I thought he was going to have me arrested, but all he said was, "Sally, when you get a chance, fax these for me."

I ran.

3: My Own Preliminary Search

I DARTED BEHIND the police station, climbed the snow bank, and tromped through the deep snow to school.

When I got there, I stopped in the bathroom and looked in the mirror. I had forgotten to change out of my jeans and to brush my hair. I also had a full milk mustache. I wiped that away with some cold water, but there was nothing I could do about my hair. My hair is dark blond and cut in a short pixie; now it was all smashed on one side where I'd been sleeping. My blue plastic glasses, which had only one leg, sat crookedly on my nose. I still had the other leg in my back pocket.

As soon as I walked into the classroom, Mrs. Jeffers called me to her desk. The kids were all doing math problems.

"You're a half hour late," she said.

"I am?" I said, because I didn't know what else to say. I stared at her big diamond ring. Even though she was young, she always dressed like a grandmother. Today she had on a gray flannel skirt and a pale pink blouse with a big floppy bow at the neck. Her hair looked like a stiff shower cap.

"Do you have any explanation?"

I said I was sorry and tried to explain about Amy being missing.

"I'm sure she'll show up. You have to worry about getting yourself where you're supposed to be, Erin. *On time*. Amy will have to take care of herself."

Then Mrs. Jeffers asked what had happened to my glasses. I told her and she helped me put the leg back on with a paper clip.

"Do you have your social studies homework?"

I pulled it out of my knapsack and put it on her desk. She looked at the smear of guinea pig poop and sighed.

"I didn't have time to copy it over," I explained.

"Go sit down, Erin. Page ninety-five in the math book. Problems one through eight."

I couldn't concentrate during math or language arts. All I could do was look out the window. I was mad that no one believed me about Amy.

Later that morning, Mrs. Jeffers squatted down beside my desk. "Did you hear a word I said about the science projects, Erin?"

I shook my head.

"Still worrying about that babysitter of yours?"

I nodded, then glanced outside again. I wished I could fly right out the window. My last report card said, "Erin is a smart girl, but she has trouble concentrating. She needs to learn to sit still." When I told Amy about that report card, she said, "Oh, that's ridiculous. Sitting still is overrated. You have the spirit of a wild animal, Erin. An eagle, maybe. Or a lynx."

Mrs. Jeffers turned to Tiffany Tran, who sat in the desk next to me. Tiffany quickly slipped the paper on which she had been drawing into her notebook.

"What about you, Tiffany? I bet you didn't hear a word, either."

Tiffany shook her head.

I looked around the room. Everyone was working in pairs. Most of the girls wore their Girl Scout uniforms. I quit Girl Scouts last year because all we ever did was indoor crafts. I wanted to go camping and exploring. I had practically memorized the sections of the Girl Scout books that had to do with exploring the outdoors or survival skills.

"Listen up, now," Mrs. Jeffers said to the two of us. "We're working in teams to design projects for the science fair. Some of the girls are killing two birds with one stone by doing projects that will get them badges."

I didn't like that expression. Why would you want to kill any birds?

Mrs. Jeffers continued, "But it doesn't look like either of you is a Girl Scout." I shook my head and so did Tiffany. "Well, then, you two can work together. Brainstorm on what we have learned about observation and documentation to design a good project."

Mrs. Jeffers left to help other students.

Tiffany wrote "observation" and "documentation" at the top of a fresh piece of paper. Then she started drawing pictures under the words and didn't even look at me.

I didn't know Tiffany very well. Most of the kids in town had been here their whole lives, like me, but Tiffany's family moved here from San Francisco at the beginning of the school year. The first two weeks of school her name was Hoa— Hoa Tran. That's a Vietnamese name. Her parents were born in Vietnam, but she was born here in the United States. A lot of the kids were curious and asked her questions, like whether she could speak Vietnamese. She always scowled and said, "I'm *American*." I guess that's why, after only two weeks of school, she changed her name to Tiffany.

I scooted my desk over next to hers and asked, "What was that picture you hid in your notebook when Mrs. Jeffers came over?"

I thought she would deny having done that, but she opened her notebook and pulled out a perfect likeness of Mrs. Jeffers. Her stiff, poofy hair and sharp chin were just right. That big floppy bow would have been hard to draw, but Tiffany had done it perfectly. Below Mrs. Jeffers's picture was the word "wanted." It looked just like the criminal pictures in the post office.

"That's good," I said.

Tiffany smiled a little bit.

"What do you think we should do our science project on?" I asked.

Tiffany shrugged and started drawing again. I stared at the words "observation" and "documentation" at the top of her sheet of paper, trying to think of a science project. I was about to ask Tiffany why she wasn't a Girl Scout, when— *Bingo!*—I had an idea.

"Let's study animal tracks in the snow," I said.

There had been a Girl Scout badge on Wildlife. I never got the badge because I didn't complete all the activities, but I loved the part about reading the signs animals leave behind. Besides, tracking animals would fit in perfectly with my *real* plans for the next day.

Tiffany finally stopped drawing. "You mean, their footprints?" she asked.

I nodded. "Tomorrow is Saturday. We could leave first thing in the morning. We could try to find lots of different kinds of animal tracks. We could *observe* what the tracks tell us about the animals."

"I could *document* the tracks by drawing them."

"Exactly."

What I didn't tell her was that I would be looking for Amy at the same time.

Having Tiffany along might not be a good idea. We would have to spend a few hours in the woods. She didn't seem like the kind of girl who liked to explore. She wore dresses every day, and her glossy black hair was always pulled back in a neat French braid, tied with a ribbon. She would probably whine a lot and slow me down.

So I revised the plan. "Maybe I could do the *observation* part in the woods. When I come home, you can help with the *documentation*."

Tiffany crossed her arms. She clenched her jaw and her nostrils flared a bit. Then she uncrossed her arms, picked up her pencil, and began drawing again.

I could tell she was mad but I didn't know why.

A second later, she put down her pencil and said, "That's a dumb idea. Documentation is taking notes and making drawings. How can I do that if I'm not there to see what there is to document?"

"Oh," I said. "Well, I guess you could come with me. If you want. But you don't have to."

She looked at me sideways. She clenched her jaw again. Then she said, "I'm coming."

I told her to meet me at nine o'clock the next morning at the intersection of the two highways. I figured she probably wouldn't show up anyway. Even if she did, she wouldn't last long. We would look around for a few minutes for tracks, then she would go home. And I'd go find the miner's cabin.

That afternoon, I ran over to the high school. Maybe Officer Foster would do a preliminary search and maybe he wouldn't. I couldn't count on it. I would do a little preliminary search of my own.

The storm still hadn't broken. A few tiny snow-flakes danced in the air, too light to fall to the ground. The sky was dark and the clouds had closed together, forming one thick blanket. If the storm developed, my parents would never let me out on Saturday.

At the high school, I asked the secretary if Amy Johnstone had been in school that day or the day before. The secretary looked at her records and said that Amy had been there Thursday but not Friday.

I thought about that. She had gone to school

on Thursday but had not come to babysit me that evening . . .

Next I ran to Amy's house, which was all the way on the other side of town. I got there just as a big moving van pulled out of the driveway. The sight of that yellow truck made my stomach somersault. Were Amy and her mother inside?

I yelled, "Hey! Hey!"

The truck turned and started to pick up speed. I pounded my hand against the bottom of the door, trying to get the driver's attention. "Hey!" I screamed.

Then I jogged away from the side of the truck so that the driver could see me out the window. Finally he slowed to a stop. He rolled down the window and glared at me, his eyebrows knit together. "What do you want?" he yelled.

"Have the Johnstones already moved to Tucson?"

"Well, we're the movers and this is their stuff."

"I mean the *people*. Mrs. Johnstone and Amy."

"Mrs. Johnstone left early yesterday morning."

"What about Amy, her daughter?"

"I wouldn't know. Look, kid, we gotta go. I'm already late."

"Do you have a phone number for them in Tucson?"

He picked up a clipboard with a bunch of yellow and white papers attached. He rustled through them. "Says here they don't have a phone hooked up yet. New apartment."

"Thank you," I said, stepping back as the truck rolled away. A terrible emptiness swelled in the middle of my rib cage. I couldn't believe that Amy would leave town without saying goodbye. I couldn't believe that she would say she could babysit and then not show up. But that obviously was what had happened. Amy had left for Tucson.

Even though it was already a long way home, I took a longcut, turning a half hour's walk into an hour's walk. The air was extra chilly, like January. Those big storm clouds sagged in the sky, releasing an occasional snowflake. The late afternoon shadows made the snow on the ground look violet, the color of wisteria blooms.

Close to home I came across some boot tracks. They led into the woods, just as the deer tracks had that morning. I wondered who had walked off into the woods and stooped down to look at the tracks. Because the snow had been on the ground for over a week, it was pretty firm. The track indent was only about two inches deep.

I looked into the woods. At this hour, about five in the afternoon, there was hardly any light left among the trees. The air in there looked black, like it would be thick to breathe. The tree limbs were dark and heavy. I thought of the time that Amy hugged the tree.

It struck me then. *Amy would not leave town without saying goodbye to me.* I was sure of it.

I didn't care if no one believed me. None of them—not Mom or Dad, not Officer Foster, and definitely not Mrs. Jeffers—knew anything about Amy. I knew she was in trouble. I was the *only* one who knew she was in trouble. Which meant it was going to have to be me who got her out of it.

4: The First Tracks

I COULD BARELY eat dinner that night. I kept thinking of the big yellow moving van, of Mrs. Johnstone in Tucson, and of Amy saying that nothing mattered. I kept thinking of the miner's cabin and my plans for finding it in the morning.

"For Pete's sake, Erin," Mom said. "Sit still."

"And finish your dinner," Dad added.

"By the way," Mom said in a softer voice. "I knew you were worried about Amy, so I drove by her house on my lunch hour. Some movers were there, loading up a big truck. So I called the Payless where Mrs. Johnstone works, and they told me she got a new job, managing her own store in Tucson."

I didn't tell Mom that I already knew all that.

"I know you liked Amy so much, honey," Mom went on. "We'll all miss her. But this is a wonderful thing for her and her mother. I bet Mrs. Johnstone will make more money. It's a good promotion."

Mom waited for me to say something, and I almost told her and Dad about the miner's cabin. I probably should have. But I didn't think they would believe me. They would be sure that Amy had gone to Tucson with her mother. Anyway, I promised Amy that I would tell no one about the cabin.

Luckily the phone rang and saved me from having to answer Mom.

Dad got up to get the phone. "Uh, yes, this is Mr. Flaherty. Yes, I'm her father," he said, glancing at me. "I see. Okay. Thank you. All right, I'll let her know." Dad hung up. He returned to the table and sat down.

"That was Officer Foster."

My ears flamed red-hot again.

"He said that he made a couple of phone calls and found out what your mother just told you. The Johnstones have moved to Tucson." Dad glanced at Mom.

Mom said, "You went to the police?"

I nodded.

"Oh, honey."

"What else did Officer Foster say?" I asked. I could tell by the expression on Dad's face that Officer Foster had said something else about me, something not very nice, maybe about my delinquency.

"Well," Dad said and paused, choosing his

words. "He said that maybe your imagination is working overtime."

I opened my mouth to argue, but the phone rang again.

This time his face tightened even more as he listened. Finally he said, "All right. Thank you for letting us know."

"That," he said, returning to the table, "was Mrs. Jeffers. It appears that you were quite late for school."

I explained about going to the police station.

"*And* that you turned in a very messy social studies report."

I explained about Dorothy's accident.

Mom and Dad looked at each other for a long time. Mom's shoulders sagged. Dad's eyes looked baggy. I could tell they were too tired to scold me. All Mom said was, "I know you're upset about Amy's leaving, honey. We'll get her address and you can write to her. But please, you must get to school on time."

I promised I would, then asked to be excused.

I pulled open the back door and stepped outside. Stars! The storm clouds had cleared away, revealing bright pinpoints of light and black space in between. The storm had been a dud.

"Yes!" I said, swinging my fist in a circle over my head. There was still a chance to find Amy.

Back inside, I took the stairs two at a time and

slammed my bedroom door behind me. Then I put my down parka, mittens, and wool hat on my desk chair for the next morning. Finally I emptied the books out of my knapsack and carried it downstairs.

Mom and Dad were drinking peppermint tea in the kitchen. I filled a water bottle and put it in the knapsack. I found the space blanket in the garage and stuffed it into my knapsack, too. Then I wrapped three energy bars in plastic and started making sandwiches.

"What are you up to?" Mom asked. "Want some peppermint tea?"

"No thanks." I explained about the science project, how Tiffany and I were going to study animal tracks in the snow.

"That's a fine project," Dad said.

"Perfect for a future vet," Mom agreed. "But not if it storms."

"It's clearing," I said. I cut the two peanut butter and honey sandwiches in half and put them in a plastic bag.

"This is supposed to be just the beginning of a series of storms," Dad warned me.

"If it's clear in the morning, can I go?"

"If it's clear, sure."

"Good," I said, and took my packed knapsack to my bedroom. I hung my I Want Privacy sign on the outside of my door. I was tired of human beings, especially adult ones, and their negative attitudes. I stroked the scratchy backs of Scoot and Ooze, but they weren't great cuddlers, so I pulled Snowball out from under the bed. She hissed. Snowball hates being disturbed, but when I lay down on the bed with her, she settled on my chest and purred.

When I woke up, Snowball was under the covers with me and a bright yellow sunlight angled in my bedroom window.

I had fallen asleep without setting my alarm. It was already eight-thirty! And I was supposed to be at the intersection at nine o'clock.

In the kitchen, Mom was sweeping up some coffee beans she'd spilled. Dad was mixing pancake batter.

"Just in time," he said. The batter made a delicious-sounding sizzle as it hit the greased pan.

"I have to meet Tiffany in thirty minutes," I warned.

"The chef will be right on it," Dad said.

Mom poured me some milk and said, "You're lucky. It's a picture-perfect day for animal tracking."

"I told you it was clearing," I said.

"You're brilliant," Dad teased. "A real clairvoyant. Just make sure you use some of that brilliance on your science project today. Don't get lost in that imagination of yours." He dumped three steaming pancakes on the plate in front of me.

"There's nothing wrong with an active imagination," Mom said.

"No," Dad agreed, "but when we have both the police and the school calling us about Erin's capers, then—"

"What are capers?" I asked.

"Shenanigans. Escapades. Adventures."

I downed my milk in two gulps. It made me mad that they thought I was just playing games.

Dad sat in the chair next to me. "Honey, all I'm saying is that you are a very smart girl. But you have to focus more on the rules. Get to school on time. Do your homework and turn in neat copies. Today I want you to pay extra attention to your science project. Don't get out there and start to play and forget all about the animal tracks, okay?"

I nodded.

"Do you have your notebook and a pencil so you can take notes?"

"Not yet."

Mom fished a small notebook and a pencil out of a kitchen drawer and tucked them in my knapsack.

"May I take my pocketknife?"

Mom and Dad had given me a pocketknife for my birthday this year, but I wasn't supposed to use it unless one of them was with me. They glanced at each other. Mom nodded slightly.

"All right," Dad said. "You know how to use it safely."

I finished my pancakes, ran to get the pocket-knife, and headed for the door. Mom caught the neck of my jacket, just like a mother cat picks up a kitten. "Not so fast, young lady. How about a kiss?" So I kissed her and Dad quickly.

"See you this afternoon." The door slammed behind me.

It was a beautiful day, the sky a deep blue and the snow sparkling as if it were covered with millions of tiny diamonds. Though the sun was bright and lemony, the air was still icy.

When I got to the intersection, it was just as I'd suspected. Tiffany was wearing saddle shoes and a long camel hair coat. Her tights-covered legs stuck out of the bottom of the coat, meaning she wore a dress—on a freezing cold Saturday! A dark green ribbon was tied to the end of her French braid.

"Hi," she said.

"Hi. You need boots and pants for walking in the snow. I don't think you can come with me. Maybe I can come over to your house later and show you what I find."

Tiffany clenched her jaw and crossed her arms

over her chest. Her nostrils flared a bit, too, just as they had in school the day before.

Then, right there beside the highway, she plunked down her knapsack and unzipped it. She yanked out a pair of jeans and pulled them on over her tights. Next she took off her coat and told me to hold it. She pulled her wool plaid dress off over her head, balled it up, and stuffed it into her knapsack. Then she put on a giant blue-and-green flannel shirt.

"Give me my coat back," she said. "I'm ready."

I looked at her shoes.

"I already tested them," she said. "The snow is packed. You can walk right on top of it."

Tiffany was certainly eager to come along. If she wanted to walk in the snow in saddle shoes, I guessed she could.

A breeze ruffled through the evergreens covering the mountains above the highway, then it ruffled through me. Clear skies usually meant colder temperatures. The snow beside the road, about five feet deep, was frozen pretty hard. Next month, in May, it would start melting fast, whole rivers running down the highway. But today it might as well have been the middle of winter.

"Let's go this way," I said, pointing in the direction Amy had shown me when she had talked about the cabin. "The animals live in the woods, away from the highway."

Tiffany climbed up the snow bank surprisingly quickly and headed into the trees.

The minute we entered the forest, a feeling as cool as the icy breeze fluttered through me. The tree trunks were black and dense, the branches heavy with snow. From here, inside the forest, it was hard to tell directions. How was I going to find that miner's cabin? What if Amy wasn't there? What if she really *had* gone to Tucson with her mother? Maybe everyone—Mom and Dad, Officer Foster, and Mrs. Jeffers—was right, after all. Maybe my imagination *was* too active.

"Tracks!" Tiffany pulled out a camera and pointed it toward a set of big round indents. Each indent had a waffle pattern inside.

"Boots," I said. "Tiffany, they're just *boots.*"

She started snapping pictures, recording the boot tracks from different angles.

Oh, boy, I thought, *is she ever dense.*

"Tiffany," I said, as she got out her sketch pad and a ruler. "These are *human* tracks."

"Duh," she said, measuring one track and taking notes. "Hmm, nine inches. Probably a female human." She scribbled something on her pad. "And only one set of tracks. A female human traveling alone."

I waited for her to finish, wondering if we would get anything done today—find Amy or do any of our assignment.

Tiffany stopped writing and said, "Erin, humans are animals, aren't they?"

"Yeah."

"Well, then why don't they count?"

"I guess you're right." I squatted down to study the tracks. They also seemed to come from the highway intersection, only from a slightly different place than where we had started. They were headed toward the mountains, deeper into the forest.

Suddenly Tiffany's words hit me: a female human traveling alone. *Amy!*

5: Telling Secrets

I HADN'T EXPECTED to find a clue so quickly. It would be a good time to review the facts. Amy disappeared on Thursday afternoon—she had been in school that day but hadn't come to baby-sit me that evening. It was now Saturday morning. No snow had fallen in that time, so her tracks wouldn't have been covered up. Also, it had been good and cold, so her tracks wouldn't have melted away, either. These could easily be Amy's tracks from Thursday afternoon.

Tiffany packed her supplies back in her knapsack and stood up. "This is fun," she said and started marching off into the woods, away from the boot tracks.

"I think we should follow these boot tracks," I said.

"Why?" Tiffany asked. "People scare away wildlife."

"She passed through two days ago. Any wildlife she scared would have come back."

"How do you know when she passed through?"

"Um, I'm just guessing," I said. "Let's just follow them for a while."

"Okay. If you want to."

We walked in silence for a few minutes. The boot tracks continued steadily away from the highway. Now and then a car or truck roared by behind us. The farther into the forest we walked, the fainter the highway sounds became. Tiffany kept slipping because there was no tread on the bottoms of her shoes.

"Tracks!" we both shouted at the sight of a new set of footprints. These crossed our path, perpendicular to the human tracks we were following. They were tiny little feet, four across. The two outside footprints were longer than the two inside footprints.

"It's a rabbit," I said. "A rabbit's two back feet come all the way up next to its two front feet when it hops."

Tiffany sketched the rabbit tracks, drawing a whole set of them across her piece of paper. As she worked, I thought of the picture she had drawn of Mrs. Jeffers.

"Don't you like Mrs. Jeffers?" I asked.

"She's okay."

"So why did you draw that picture of her and write 'wanted' under it?"

"I was practicing."

"Practicing what?"

"I'm going to be a police artist when I grow up."

Tiffany photographed the rabbit tracks. She said, "Sometimes when there's been a crime, the victim has to describe what the perpetrator— that's the criminal—looks like. An artist has to draw a picture of him based on the victim's description. That's what I'm going to do. That kind of drawing is called a composite.

"You want to help with these tracks?" she asked. She handed me the ruler. "Take measurements."

Even though I didn't like her telling me what to do, I measured the rabbit tracks, front feet and back feet, and called out the figures. She wrote them down.

Then she stood up and said, "We're doing pretty well. We have two kinds of tracks already."

"Yeah," I said, annoyed. She was doing all the documenting.

"Let's follow the rabbit tracks and discover where it lives." She marched off.

"I want to follow the human tracks," I insisted.

Tiffany stopped and turned around. She plunked her hands on her hips. "I want to follow the *rabbit* tracks."

"Then you go ahead," I said. "I'm going this way." The animal tracks were my idea, after all.

Besides, we could still hear the highway, just barely, and she might as well go back now. I wasn't stopping until I found the miner's cabin.

I turned my back and walked in the direction of the boot tracks. A second later, snow crunched behind me. Tiffany was running to catch up. Just as she got near me, she landed hard on her behind.

"Why do you keep trying to get rid of me? Mrs. Jeffers said we were supposed to work in teams. You just want to do it all yourself."

"*You're* the one who's doing it all yourself," I argued. "All you do is tell me what to do."

Tiffany's hair was coming out of the French braid and was blowing around her face in wisps. Her big camel hair coat was dusted with crunchy snow. I gave her a hand and pulled her up.

"Come on," I said. "I can't tell you why, but I have a really good reason for wanting to follow these human tracks, okay?"

"Okay," she said. "What's the reason?"

"I just *said* I couldn't tell you."

Why wouldn't she go home!

"Okay," she said cheerfully. "So what are *you* going to be when you grow up?"

"A vet."

"Do you have a dog?"

"No, but I have a cat, a guinea pig, two fish, and two snakes."

"My parents won't let me have pets."

"Why not?"

"Too messy."

"Do your parents make you wear dresses every day?"

"Yes. They think I'm at the library today."

"You're going to get in trouble if they find out you're not."

"I don't care. They don't let me do anything. They were this way when we lived in San Francisco, too, but here in the mountains they're even worse. They think a bear will get me walking down Main Street."

I laughed, but Tiffany didn't think it was funny. She said, "My mom is always so sad. She grew up in a war, so she thinks everything will be taken away at any minute."

"You mean the Vietnam war?"

Tiffany nodded. "She's afraid of anything I do. My brother is so lucky. He's going to college next year. Then he'll get to do anything he wants. This is my brother's shirt," she said, pulling the flannel collar out of the neck of her coat.

"I wish I had a brother," I said. "Or even better, a sister. I live alone with my parents."

"And your animals."

"Yeah." It was nice that Tiffany remembered them.

A loud whoosh made me jump. Then we heard

a heavy thumping. Tiffany clutched my arm. The white tail of a deer, centered in a tawny rump, disappeared into the forest.

"What's that?" Tiffany squeaked.

"It's just a deer, silly," I said.

"It looked so big."

"Haven't you seen a deer before?"

"Only from the car."

"Let's go look at its tracks."

It was growing colder. I couldn't hear the highway at all anymore. My watch said ten-thirty. We must have walked at least two miles.

A breeze ruffled through the branches of the trees and puffy white clouds floated overhead like barges in a sea of blue sky. They looked like friendly clouds, but I remembered what Dad had said about storms coming.

"Look," I said, "since you're getting scared, maybe you'd better go back."

"By myself?"

"It's not far," I said.

Tiffany stared at me for so long, *I* started to feel scared. Finally she said, "You're crazy. First of all, I am not scared. The deer just startled me. Second of all, no one should hike alone in the woods."

She was right. I remember reading about the buddy system in one of my Girl Scout books.

Tiffany leaned forward. "And you better tell me

right now your reason for wanting to follow these boot tracks."

"I can't tell you that."

"Erin Flaherty, you're stuck-up and sneaky!"

"Then go home! Or to the library where you're supposed to be!"

She took a step toward me. "I'm not walking out alone. You have to come with me."

I didn't know what to do. She was right, but I couldn't abandon Amy. Not now. Not when I was almost there. How far could the miner's cabin be, anyway? Another half hour at the most. The sky was more white than blue, although the clouds still looked friendly. But for how long? There might not be enough time to walk Tiffany back to the highway and then return to find Amy, not if a storm gathered.

Tiffany saw me eyeing the boot tracks again. "Tell me why you want to follow the boot tracks. You have to."

"I do not have to," I said, but then I decided I'd better tell her at least part of the story. "My babysitter is missing. I thought up the animal tracks idea so that I could go look for her."

"You mean she's a missing person?" Tiffany's face brightened. "Like the kids on the milk cartons?"

I nodded, remembering that she wanted to be a police artist.

"But why do you think she's out *here?* Why do you think these are *her* tracks?"

"I have verbal evidence. Amy made some statements that lead me to believe she's out here."

Tiffany studied me for a moment with that stubborn look on her face. There was no way she'd go home alone. I didn't have a choice: if I was going to look for Amy, I'd have to take Tiffany.

So I told her everything—what Amy had told me about the miner's cabin, how sad she was about moving, and about my going to the police, the high school, and Amy's house. I told her how no one believed me.

"They're probably right," I said by the time I finished. "She's probably not out here at all. I bet she went to Tucson with her mother."

"Wait a minute! Wait a minute!" Tiffany cried. "Go over again what the mover and the school secretary said."

I repeated what I'd told her. Then Tiffany said, "The mover said Mrs. Johnstone left for Tucson Thursday *morning*. But the school secretary said that Amy was in school on Thursday, right?"

Tiffany was smart. Amy couldn't have gone with her mother to Tucson on Thursday morning if she had been in school that day.

"Still," I said, "would Army really have come out *here?*"

Tiffany thought for a moment, then said, "My mom says Vietnam is the most beautiful place in the world. She gets so sad about home that she does really strange things sometimes. I've never met Amy. But if she was as sad as you say she was, and if she talked about coming out here, then maybe she did."

Tiffany didn't think my reasoning was wacky. Maybe her imagination was as active as mine. Or maybe, just maybe, we were right.

"Can I come with you to look for her?" Tiffany asked. "I'm *not* scared."

I didn't really have a choice. Besides, Tiffany was the only one who believed me. "Okay," I said.

She grinned, revealing deep dimples on either side of her mouth. "Hold still," she said, running ahead of me and turning around. "I need some pictures of the wildlife." She snapped a picture of me. The camera covered the top half of her face, but below it I could see her grin. That was the first time I had ever heard Tiffany Tran crack a joke. I made a face for the camera.

We set out again, following the tracks. Not more than fifteen minutes later, they led us to a place where the trees opened up into a pretty snow-covered meadow. Sunlight, spilling from the breaks in the clouds, hit patches of the meadow, making the snow a harsh white. Other parts of the meadow were enveloped in shadow and glowed a deep blue.

"It's so quiet," Tiffany said.

It was more than quiet, it was totally silent. Sometimes, out in the woods like that, you can actually hear silence. It was spooky.

"Let's eat," I said loudly, then made a lot of noise getting into my knapsack.

We took out the space blanket, folded it in half, and spread it out on the snow. I was so hungry I could have eaten both of my peanut butter and honey sandwiches. Tiffany had two big balls of rice, which she ate facing away from me. At school, she always tried to hide her lunch by eating behind a big book or turning her back to the rest of the kids.

"Why do you hide your lunches?" I asked.

She scowled. "No one else eats rice for lunch."

"Maybe you could trade. Eduardo always trades his tacos for Sam's sandwiches."

"Who wants to eat rice balls?"

"Here." I held out my second sandwich. "Trade."

Tiffany hesitated, then handed me a rice ball. I thought it was going to taste bland, like plain rice does, but it was flavored with something yummy. "This is good," I said.

By the time we finished eating, the puffy white clouds had grown together and become one big storm cloud covering the whole sky. It was the color of gunmetal, gray and flat. And it was perfectly still and quiet. The wind had died completely.

I looked over my shoulder at our tracks. They would be easy to follow back to the highway when we were ready. There were still plenty more hours of daylight.

"Do you think the miner's cabin is nearby?" Tiffany asked.

"Probably," I said. "Let's go."

The boot tracks headed across the meadow. When we reached the far side, we stopped to rest for a moment, and I heard a gentle gurgling sound.

"What's that?" Tiffany asked.

We both looked around and saw nothing—except for a very gray sky and, because there was no more sunlight, gray snow to match.

Then a rumble that seemed to come from right beneath our feet made both of us jump.

"A stream," I said. "There's a stream running below us. Right under our feet. The rumble is stones being moved along by the water."

"Maybe we'd better get off the ice," Tiffany suggested.

"Good idea."

We couldn't see where the stream was, because, like the rest of the meadow, it was covered with snow. We moved forward quickly until we couldn't hear the sounds beneath our feet.

Then we continued following the tracks to an enormous cedar tree on the border of the meadow. The tree had a big skirt of branches that reached out and down, touching the snow. The boot tracks disappeared under the skirt of branches.

Whoever's tracks these were had crawled under the branches. That person might be in there right now.

"Amy?" I whispered, glancing around at the meadow, now completely wrapped in dark shadow.

"Do you think she's in there?" Tiffany asked, also whispering.

"Amy?" I tried to speak up. "Is that you?"

6: The Saddle Shoe Problem

I CREPT SLOWLY toward the skirt of branches. If Amy was in there, wouldn't she have heard us by now? Wouldn't she have called out?

Maybe she was unconscious. Maybe she got too cold, or too hungry, and passed out. After all, she had been out here almost forty-eight hours by now.

"Hello?" I called softly. "Anyone in there?"

No answer.

Tiffany gripped the back of my down parka. I turned and looked at her.

"I'm *not* scared," she whispered fiercely.

"I'm going to look inside," I whispered back, then wondered why we were whispering.

I moved to the tip of the nearest cedar branch. It had been growing in that position for a long, long time and was hard to lift. I got down on my hands and knees and used my shoulder to heave the branch up. Eventually I was able to push my head into the tree shelter.

For a moment I couldn't see anything. It was too dark. Slowly, my eyes adjusted, and I could make out the huge trunk and a bed of cedar needles, completely dry because they were protected by the overhanging branches. The needles were all scuffed up, as if someone had been in there, all right. There was a big round indent in the needles, like a nest. At the moment, though, the cedar-tree fort was empty.

"There's no one in here," I called back, feeling disappointed. I worked my way out from under the branches, moving backward on all fours.

When I stood up and shook out my legs, I didn't see Tiffany. "Hey!" I yelled. "Hey, Tiffany!"

"I'm over here," her voice called from the other side of the cedar. "Come look."

Tiffany pointed at more boot tracks. She said, "It looks like she—if it was Amy—crawled out from this side. The tracks go on."

So they did. The tracks headed into the trees on this side of the meadow. I didn't like the idea of going back into the trees. This forest looked even darker and thicker than the one on the other side of the meadow.

Besides, it was starting to snow.

Again I felt pulled in two directions. It was clear we should go back. But how could I desert Amy? Just the thought of Officer Foster's brushy mustache and hairy ears made me decide against going back to the police station. Same thing with Mrs. Jeffers's stiff hairdo and pointy chin. Even Dad said "Erin's capers," as if I were just a silly goose. None of them believed me.

If I found Amy, I could prove them all wrong.

"We have to hurry," I said, marching forward into the woods, following the tracks once again. "The weather's getting worse."

The miner's cabin had to be close by. It had to be.

"Where'd the tracks go?" I asked a few minutes later. "They disappeared."

"That's because the snow is so hard here," Tiffany pointed out.

She was right. We'd been climbing in elevation, slowly but steadily. That meant colder temperatures, which meant the snow on the ground was frozen harder. Here, where the tracks seemed to end, the snow was covered with a crust of ice.

I explained about the elevation, and Tiffany added, "Also, the forest over here is denser than on the other side of the meadow. Less sunlight gets through to soften the snow."

"Good observation," I said.

"Look for other signs of a person passing through," she suggested, "like broken twigs."

"Okay. Maybe the snow will be softer a bit beyond and we can pick up the tracks again."

I walked gingerly across the ice. Even in my

boots, it was slippery, so I wasn't surprised when Tiffany, in her slick saddle shoes, took a spill.

I helped her up and we continued, me walking and Tiffany skating, but the crust of ice didn't end. We didn't see any more boot tracks at all, and the forest was darkening by the minute. It was only two o'clock, but it looked like dusk. Now I *knew* we had to go back.

I turned, planning to tell Tiffany that we had to give up, just in time to see her legs fly from beneath her. She hit the ice face first and lay there, sprawled.

I hurried over to her. "Are you all right?"

She used her arms to push herself into a sitting position and brushed the dirty, crusty ice off her face. "My ankle," she moaned. "I twisted my ankle."

"Can you stand?"

"I don't know." I helped her to her feet and she tried to put weight on the ankle. "Ouch!"

Think, I told myself. *What have I read about sprains?*

Out loud, I said, "The Junior Girl Scout handbook says not to move a person with a sprain and to call a doctor or hospital. At least that's what I think it says."

Tiffany rolled her eyes. "Great. Do you see a pay phone nearby?"

Then I remembered when Mom had fallen on

our walkway and sprained her wrist. Dad had her ice it for a half hour at a time. The icing brought down the swelling.

I took out my space blanket. "Sit on this and take off your shoe and sock."

By stomping hard with my boot, I was able to break through the crust of ice to the soft snow underneath. I put several big handfuls in the plastic sandwich bag. "Hold this on your ankle."

"I didn't think you were a Girl Scout," Tiffany said.

"I used to be. I quit. I like the badge book and the handbook, though."

"I quit, too."

"You did?"

"Yeah. I was in a troop in San Francisco, but all we ever did was public service, like serve food in soup kitchens and clean houses for elderly people. I mean, that was okay, but I wanted to do art projects, too."

"Really? All my troop did was crafts. I wanted to do the outdoors stuff."

Tiffany grinned at me. "I guess we're both Girl Scout dropouts."

I grinned back.

She said, "I still have the books, too. Mainly I looked at the pictures, though. I didn't read much of it."

"Let's see if you can walk."

I helped Tiffany get up. She put some weight on her foot. "Aaah!" she yelped. She slumped back down to the space blanket. I sat next to her. How were we going to get out of here if Tiffany couldn't walk?

I pulled my pocketknife out and opened the blade.

Tiffany said, "Don't touch my foot with that!"

"I wasn't going to. I'm thinking about cutting a branch and making you a crutch. Do you think the snow is firm enough for a crutch to work?"

"It would be better than nothing," she said.

I searched for a branch that was strong and straight, with a forked end. It took me a long time to find it, and when I did, I didn't know how I would get to it. The branch was several feet above my head on a Douglas fir.

Grabbing a lower branch, I swung my legs up. I couldn't resist hanging by my knees for a minute. "Hey, Tiffany!" I shouted, swinging back and forth like a monkey. She giggled.

Then I grasped the tree branch, swung myself up, and climbed until I could finally reach my crutch branch. While holding on to the tree trunk with one arm, I opened my knife blade with my free hand. The branch was about an inch in diameter and my knife wasn't very big, so I had to slice away the wood, bit by bit. Finally the branch fell to the snow with a satisfying thunk.

Dragging my branch back to Tiffany, I pretended I was a prehistoric woman and that my down parka was really an animal skin. But the seriousness of our situation made it hard for me to play for very long.

It was snowing now, but the dense canopy of the forest caught most of the snow far above our heads. Even so, if it started snowing harder, or if a wind came up, the snow would come right through the canopy. Besides, it would be dark in another couple of hours. We had to get moving soon.

I carved the greenery off the branch, then cut back the forked end so that each side was about six inches long. Tiffany stood up on one foot so that I could judge how much to cut off the bottom of the crutch. Finally I sharpened that end so that it would hold better on the ice.

Tiffany put her shoe back on and tried walking with the crutch. "It helps a lot," she said. "I can walk if I don't have to put my full weight on my ankle."

"There's one more thing I'd better do," I said, "but you'll probably get in trouble for it."

"Aren't we already in trouble?" Tiffany asked.

"Yeah. Give me the bottoms of your feet. There's no way you're going to be able to walk with that crutch, your bad ankle, and those slippery soles. I'm going to cut tread into your saddle shoes."

Tiffany sat right down on the space blanket and held up her left foot. I cut narrow trenches, about an eighth of an inch wide, into the rubber on the bottoms of her saddle shoes, in both directions. When I was done, the soles looked more like the waffle bottoms of boots.

"We'd better go," I said, putting the space blanket back in my knapsack.

Tiffany put one arm around my shoulder and put the crutch under her other arm. "The tread works great," she said. "Let's pretend we're in the Antarctic, trekking to the South Pole. My leg froze off and we have to do the whole thing by—"

"Tiffany," I said, "we're in enough trouble in *real* life." Talk about an active imagination!

"Oh." She sounded disappointed.

"We have a long way to go before dark."

"When's dark?"

I looked at my watch. "In about an hour."

It was slow going. By the time we reached the meadow again, it was dusk. And snowing, hard. A stiff wind swept the snow in great swirls above the meadow. I couldn't even see the forest on the other side.

I knew than that we would never make it back to the highway.

7: Predator and Prey

TIFFANY LIMPED ACROSS the meadow, through the blowing snow, as best she could. Even if it seemed impossible, I didn't know what else to do but try to get back to the highway.

Everything was white, absolutely white. There was nothing to see but flying snowflakes. It was much colder, too, because the wind had a big bite. Walking made me warm, though, and the contrast of my warm face with the cold air fogged up my glasses. It was like walking blind.

It was then that I realized what we had to do. If we tried to walk out in a blizzard, we would get lost. It had taken us well over two hours—not counting all our stops—to get here in good weather, daylight, and with four strong ankles. It could take us three or four times that long now. We wouldn't get out before dark. We'd get very wet from the snow. We had to find somewhere in the forest, somewhere dry, to spend the night.

The wind was howling so loudly now that it was hard to be heard. I shouted to Tiffany, "We're going back. To the forest."

She made that face of hers, the stubborn one where her nostrils flare and her jaw clenches. "Okay," she said, understanding, and turned around.

As she limped back toward the woods, she yelled, "This is all my fault. I'm sorry."

But she was wrong. It wasn't her fault. The whole day had been my idea. I was the one who insisted we keep going, even as the weather changed, because I wanted to find Amy.

"It's not your fault," I shouted back. "Besides, I'm glad I'm not alone out here."

Then I had an idea.

"Hey," I said. "Remember the cedar tree? The one with the heavy branches that reach down to the ground? It was perfectly dry in there. We could stay there for the night."

"*If* we can find it again."

"Sure. It's right on the edge of the forest."

But when we got back to the forest, we didn't see it. We walked a long way in one direction, then a long way in the other. How could such a big tree disappear?

"I have to rest a minute," Tiffany said. Her ankle was really bothering her. She grabbed a big snow-covered tree branch. White snow swirled all around us We could hardly see a thing.

"Hey," Tiffany said, shaking the branch she was holding. "Isn't *this* our tree?"

I squatted down and examined the lower branches. Sure enough, the thick mesh of branches reached down and touched the ground.

"Good observation," I said, lifting my mittened hand for a high five. She slapped it and almost fell off the crutch.

"Whoa," I said, steadying her. "Let's go inside."

I dove in first and held the heavy branch up while Tiffany crawled in after me. Then I scooted over to the other side of the trunk to brush the snow off my parka. That way our side would stay dry.

"This side of the trunk is our porch," I told Tiffany. "Come brush your coat off over here."

"Totally cool," she said. "This is the coolest fort I've ever seen."

She was right. The bed of cedar needles was scratchy but dry and cushiony. The whole tree smelled sweet and fresh. Occasionally a really strong gust of wind pushed through the branches, but mostly it was quiet and calm inside our fort. I took off my glasses and polished them on my shirt.

We each had a drink of water. Then I crawled to the edge of the fort, reached under the branches, and scooped some snow into the water bottle to keep it full. I had learned this trick from Dad. As long as there's lots of water in the bottle, added snow will melt. That's why you have to do it every time you drink.

"Are you scared?" I asked Tiffany.

"No," she said firmly. Then she added, "Sometimes when I start to feel scared, I pretend the scary thing is something different. Like all that snow falling? I decided that the earth is dressing up to go to a ball. The snow is a big, soft, elegant cape she's throwing on. Then it's not so scary."

"I think you would like Amy," I said. "She says that trees give the best hugs."

"Then I guess we're in a good place."

"I guess so."

We both snuggled up closer to the cedar trunk.

Thinking of Amy made me feel blue. Was she in her miner's cabin? Was she in Tucson? Was she safe? She knew things like how trees are good huggers, but did she know how to build a fire?

One day during spring break, when Amy was still pretending that she was going to the prom with Justin, she wanted to practice dancing. I didn't know how to dance, so she said she would teach me. She went through all of Mom and Dad's tapes, saying "Yuck" and "I can't believe they listen to this junk," until she found some old Beatles tapes. "These are good," she said.

We danced for two hours that afternoon. She

showed me a bunch of moves. I laughed so hard my stomach felt like it would explode.

Finally our neighbor came over and pounded on the door. She said that she had been calling us on the phone for an hour, but we had the music up so loud we didn't hear. We stopped dancing then.

"What's the point if you can't feel the music?" Amy told me. "When you dance, you've got to feel the beat all through your bones."

We were both so hot from dancing, we were drenched in sweat. "Come on," Amy said, "let's go cool off." She ran right out the back door and flopped down in the snow. Then she lay there smiling, in nothing but jeans and a T-shirt.

"Come on, come on!" she called, but I didn't throw myself in the snow. She lay there until she was shaking really hard from the cold and her bare arms were as red as tomatoes.

I pulled and pulled on her arm until she finally got up and came inside. I brewed hot peppermint tea and made her wear Mom's fleece jacket until she warmed up.

I liked that part, too. I liked doing things for Amy as much as I liked having fun with her. Spring break was just like magic. The neighbor never told Mom and Dad. No matter what Amy and I did that week, we didn't get in trouble.

But we were in trouble now.

"I'm hungry," Tiffany said after a while. We sat with our backs against the cedar trunk, our legs crossed. "I have a bag of M&M's and an apple. Should we pool our food?"

Her M&M's sounded so good, but all I had were energy bars. Mom made them out of dates, nuts, seeds, honey, and lots of other stuff. Dad thought they were disgusting, but Mom and I liked them.

"I have three energy bars, but you'd better try one before you agree to share your M&M's."

She ignored my suggestion and pulled open the bag, then poured M&M's into her lap. She divided them evenly and handed me a pile. "Here," she said.

"Thanks."

"Um, Erin?"

"Yeah?"

"I didn't mean it when I said you're stuck-up."

"That's okay," I said. "I'm sorry I was trying to get rid of you."

"Okay," she said.

Then I felt sort of embarrassed, so I started eating M&M's. I ate mine slowly, savoring each chocolate piece.

After that, we were still hungry, so we each ate an energy bar. Tiffany said hers was good, but I could tell she had trouble swallowing it. We agreed to save the last energy bar and the apple for breakfast.

"After that's gone," Tiffany said, "we'll have to hunt for our food."

"Don't be silly," I said. "We'll hike out in the morning. Your ankle will be better, the storm will clear, and we'll follow our tracks back to the road."

"Oh," she said softly, as if she was disappointed, as if she *wanted* to stay out here.

I crawled over to the edge of the branches and pulled them apart to look. The snow fell in big, thick flakes. In the little bit of light left in the sky, I saw the smooth indents of our tracks leading into the fort. They were quickly filling with snow. Even if Tiffany's ankle and the weather were better in the morning, our tracks would be gone, covered by the blanket of fresh snow. How would we find the highway through the forest?

Tiffany said, "Okay, let's pretend we're lost deep in the wilds of Alaska. We have to live off the land until we're rescued. What would we eat?"

In the dimming light I could still see the small dimples that dotted each side of her smile. Her eyebrows were raised, waiting for my answer. So I said, "How about roast squirrel with pine pitch sauce?"

"Yum," she said. "I'll make delicious rabbit brochettes marinated in mashed berries."

"This is making me hungrier," I complained. Then I added, "How about a side dish of sautéed roots with mushroom gravy?"

"A salad of forest greens with bark croutons!"

"And for dessert, we'll have snow flavored with bee honey."

"I can hardly see anymore," Tiffany said. "Do you think there are any predators out here?"

"Sure. Lots."

"Like what?"

"Bear, coyote, maybe mountain lion."

That quieted Tiffany for a moment. Then she asked, "What's their prey?"

"Bears are omnivores."

"That means they eat everything."

"Coyotes are carnivorous."

"Meat," Tiffany said thoughtfully. "What kind of meat?"

"How does your ankle feel?" I asked, trying to change the subject.

But I only made it worse, because she said, "I read that wolves go after the young and lame members of herds."

"Well, we're too far south for wolves and we're not a herd. I don't think any wild animals are going to eat us."

"Okay." The word was tiny in her throat. I had begun to think that nothing scared her, but apparently the thought of predators and prey did. Maybe she'd heard too much from her mother about bears on Main Street.

"We should ice your ankle again." I scooted

over to the edge of the fort and refilled the sandwich bag with snow. Tiffany put it on her sore ankle. Then we sat in silence as the cedar-tree fort, and all the world around it, became perfectly black with the stormy night.

When Tiffany finished icing her ankle, we lay down, curled up together like two bear cubs to stay warmer. I left my glasses on so that I wouldn't lose them.

"Maybe we should tell stories," Tiffany said.

"Good idea. You start."

"Well . . . ," Tiffany said, thinking. Then she was quiet. She had fallen asleep.

I snuggled down into the cedar needles and up against Tiffany's big wool coat, thinking of my bedroom and all my animals, especially Snowball and her thick, warm fur. A big ball of tears rose in my chest, so I squeezed my eyes tight and pushed the thoughts out of my mind. Luckily, I was as tired as Tiffany and also drifted off to sleep.

I don't know how long I slept. A strange feeling woke me up. When I opened my eyes, the tree fort was pitch dark. After blinking hard a couple of times, I noticed pinpoints of silvery light coming from tiny openings in the branches. Something made me look over to the edge of the fort. There, peeking beneath the skirt of branches, were two glassy eyes, like marbles.

8: As Wild as the Animals

I STARED BACK at the eyes. I wanted to wake up Tiffany, but was too afraid to speak or even move. I nudged her a bit, but she only sighed and curled into a tighter ball.

The eyes were too big to belong to a rabbit or a chipmunk. It could be a big hungry bear just coming out of hibernation. This was the time of year they're the hungriest. Or it could be a coyote—just wild dogs, Amy had said, but even tame dogs can get really mean if provoked.

Then I thought: What if the eyes belonged to the boot tracks? What if they were *human* eyes?

Could it be Amy? Why would she be wandering in the night? Had she maybe lost her mind? If it were Amy, wouldn't she have spoken?

Tiffany's body jerked. She had awakened and seen the eyes, too. She sat up quickly.

The creature snarled, and we both screamed.

The eyes disappeared.

Tiffany and I sat clutching each other, listening, but I didn't hear another sound: no crunching on snow, no heavy breathing, no flapping. The animal had vanished silently.

"What was that?" Tiffany finally whispered.

"I don't know."

"Do you think it's out there right now, waiting for us?"

"I don't know."

I didn't mention my thought that they could have been human eyes. Somehow that was the most terrifying of all.

I prepared to spend the rest of the night sitting up and definitely awake. I wasn't about to go back to sleep, not with that . . . animal . . . stalking our shelter.

It was very cold, so I spread the space blanket over our legs. It helped a bit. Still, I felt so dismal. I tried to block out thoughts of Mom and Dad, but it was hard. They would think I had gone searching for animal tracks in the woods behind town, not out here by the highway intersection. They had no idea where we were.

Bright spots still glowed through the tiny openings in the branches. I decided to have a look outside.

The sky had cleared completely and there was a giant moon, nearly full. That was the source of the silvery light coming through the branches. I was able to look at my watch in the light of the moon: only two o'clock. We had hours before daylight.

"Did you see it?" Tiffany asked. She meant the creature.

"No. It's not here anymore."

As I sat back against the trunk, I heard Tiffany rummaging in her knapsack. "Here, feel this."

I felt a very soft fabric that covered something lumpy.

"It's my magic bag," she said. "It's blue velvet. I'm going to show you what's inside. But since it's too dark to see, we're going to do it by touch. Sometimes I like to draw things just by feel. Here."

She placed what I could tell was a seashell in my hand.

"My best friend in San Francisco gave it to me. Put it up to your ear," she said. "Can you hear the ocean?"

The shell was too small to hear the ocean in it, but I held it up to my ear anyway and said, "Yeah, I hear it."

"I bet you can't guess what this is." She handed me a small cylinder.

When I shook it, something inside swished back and forth. "I give up."

She said, "It's sand from a beach in Vietnam. My mom gathered it before she and my dad moved to the United States."

I held the little glass jar up to my ear and shook it again. "Wow," I said.

"One last thing."

This time I could tell that what she handed me was a stone.

"My brother is going to be a physicist. He studies the tiniest particles that exist in the universe. He says that there are whole universes in each stone like this. He gave it to me. It's a yellow agate."

"Do you carry your magic bag with you everywhere?"

"Most of the time. When we get home, we can make one for you."

"Okay." I liked holding the yellow agate. It grew warm in my fist. "You know what?" I said. "I thought you would be real whiny in the outdoors."

"Now you know I'm not," Tiffany said.

"Yeah," I said sleepily. I pinched myself, not wanting to fall asleep, not with wild animals—or worse—roaming the forest. But holding Tiffany's magic rock comforted me, and soon, still sitting up, I slept again.

When Tiffany shook me awake, it took me a minute to remember where I was. When I did, I felt a hammer of fear in my chest. I had meant to stay awake! I had meant to keep watch! A filmy light was filling the shelter. I was starving.

"Let's eat breakfast," Tiffany said.

"Okay."

We used the pocketknife to cut the apple and the last energy bar in halves. Eating, even that little bit, warmed me up.

By the time we finished, bright spots showed through the branches.

I pulled apart two branches. The sky was a brilliant blue! The meadow was covered with a blanket of fresh snow, gently glowing in the early morning light. It was so pretty, I felt better instantly.

"Come on," I said. "It's a beautiful day. We can go home!"

I crawled out and gave Tiffany a hand. She stood up, her crutch propped under one arm, and smiled.

"How's your ankle?" I asked.

Gingerly, she set it down on the snow and put a little weight on it. Her smile brightened. "Better," she said. "It still hurts, but it's much better."

I looked around the meadow. Of course, our footprints were completely covered by the four inches of fresh snow but there were other tracks. . . .

"Look, Tiffany." The tracks ran right up to our tree, then turned around and went back out into the meadow. They looked a lot like the tracks Snowball had made the summer before in the freshly poured patio cement. Only these were a *lot* bigger.

"Bobcat," I whispered.

"Wow," Tiffany said, unzipping her knapsack. She pulled out her notepad, pencil, and ruler.

"Want to know the difference between dog and cat tracks?" I asked.

She nodded.

"Cats hold their claws in when they walk, but dogs can't. So if the claws show in the prints, they're dog tracks."

Tiffany sketched the tracks. "That means those were bobcat eyes staring in at us."

"Yep." I remembered how when I first had looked in the cedar-tree fort, there had been a big round indent in the fallen needles, like a nest. "You know what, Tiffany? I think we just slept in a bobcat den."

She stopped sketching for a second. *"Really?"*

"Yep."

"She must have been mad to find us in her bed!"

I didn't like to think about what she could have done to kick us out.

"Here," Tiffany said, handing me her camera, "you take the pictures." She began measuring the size of the tracks.

"Are you serious?"

"We still have to do our science project," she

said. "Now we have human, rabbit, deer, and bobcat. We'll get a blue ribbon in the science fair for sure."

"*If* we get out of here alive."

She looked at me, surprised, as if she had never thought of that. Then she said, "Well, if we do get out of here alive, we'd better have a good reason for having been here."

"And you think our parents are going to think a science fair project is a good enough reason for staying overnight in the wilderness?"

"No," Tiffany admitted, "but finding Amy is a pretty good one."

"But . . . ," I started, then stopped.

Tiffany finished her measurements, notes, and sketches, then tucked her things back in her knapsack.

"But," I started again, "we have to go back to the highway now. We can't find Amy. Our parents are going to be so worried."

Tiffany leaned on her crutch and scowled. Then, after a minute, she smiled. "Okay," she said. "But the minute we get home, I'll do a composite drawing of Amy. You can tell me all the details of what she looks like. We'll copy the drawing and post it all over town. Also, we'll go back to the police station. This time we'll *make* them come look for her out here. Okay?"

"Okay," I said, wondering again if I was even

right about Amy's being out here. And if I was right, could I just leave her now? I thought again of my parents, though, and knew we had to go home as quickly as possible.

"Let's go," I said. "I'm so hungry. Maybe my dad will make pancakes for both of us when we get home."

I knew I was going to get a lot more than pancakes when I got home, but I'd worry about that later. First we had to find the highway. And to do that, we had to cross the ice-covered stream again.

Tiffany's ankle was better, but she was slow. The crutch wasn't much help in the fresh snow; it punched right through. When we could hear the stream gurgling below the surface of the snow, we stopped. I wondered if she should use the crutch as she crossed. It might break the ice. But if I helped her across, there would be double weight on the ice. Better to go one at a time.

We couldn't tell exactly where the stream began. The snow covered everything, but there was a small slope that was probably the bank down to the water. Tiffany took a deep breath and shuffled across, leaning on her crutch.

Then I went. I could hear the water sliding below the snow and ice under my feet. I slipped but stayed upright and kept walking, reaching the other side in a few seconds.

I took Tiffany's arm to help her walk, and we continued on. As we loped across the meadow, the long shadows pulled back from the surrounding mountains. Then, just as we reached the far side, the sun burst over the top of the mountain to the east. The fresh-fallen snow glittered. A bunch of birds began singing all at once.

We entered the forest. From here I knew it was about a two-hour walk back to the highway. The only problem was, there were no tracks to follow. We would just have to go forward and hope to get there.

We walked and walked and walked. Almost all of Tiffany's hair had fallen out of her braid. Clumps of it hung in her face, and she had a big smudge of dirt across one cheek.

My own short hair felt like a bird's nest, tangled with little pieces of tree bark in it. My glasses had a streak of pine pitch across one lens that I couldn't wipe off.

We were beginning to look as wild as the animals.

I was also feeling tired and weak. Trudging through fresh snow was hard work, even if it was only four inches deep.

Then I saw a brightness through the trees, which meant open space ahead. The open space could only be one thing—the highway!

I didn't hear any traffic, but it was Sunday

morning now, and there was never much traffic then. We'd been walking for only two hours, but maybe we had come a more direct route this time. After all, even if Tiffany was real slow, we weren't stopping and taking pictures as we had before. I strained my ears, hoping to hear a car.

I thought of pancakes swimming in maple syrup and a steaming mug of peppermint tea. I thought of big hugs from Mom and Dad. Those thoughts helped me push on to the edge of the forest.

I couldn't wait to see that plowed highway.

Then we were standing at the edge of the forest. And before us . . . a snow-covered meadow.

There were tracks in the meadow, human tracks, a pair of them. To one side of the tracks were holes, about an inch and a half in diameter—Tiffany's crutch.

We were back at the same meadow in which we'd spent the night.

9: Building Our Camp

"I'M NOT STAYING in that bobcat den again," Tiffany said.

"It might be the only shelter," I said. We were too tired to keep looking for the highway. Without our old tracks to follow, we'd just keep going in circles.

"What time is it?"

The sun was directly above our heads. "Noon."

"Let's build a fire and send smoke signals."

"Good idea," I said. "And it'll keep us warm."

"I'm not getting back in that bobcat den," Tiffany said again.

"Okay," I said. "If we can build a fire, maybe that will keep us warm enough. As long as it doesn't storm again."

For now, the sky was clear and blue, but it could cloud up in a second. Then we would *have* to go back into the bobcat den. So I insisted on building our fire not too far from the den, just in case we needed it.

"I'm not getting in it," Tiffany said, as she carefully crossed the stream for the third time.

When I got about halfway across the covered stream, I heard a loud crunch—the ice below my feet sank—then a slurping sound. I leapt quickly, hoping to reach the bank.

Safe! I turned around to look. A blue pool of water formed in the depression where my boots had cracked the ice! The bright April sun was melting the thick ice covering the stream.

We found a spot on the edge of the meadow— a good distance form the bobcat den. We were near the forest but enough in the open to be seen from the sky. The snow was too deep to clear away, but if we built a fire *on* the snow, it would melt the snow and put itself out.

We'd have to build the fire on a bed of green branches. Hopefully, it wouldn't burn through them.

As I cut the greenery with my knife, Tiffany hobbled into the dense forest to search for twigs to use as kindling.

A cold wind swept across the meadow. As long as I kept moving, I was warm, but my arms and legs were so tired, they felt like bags of sand. We had to build this fire. It was our only hope—both for being rescued and for staying warm. Even with the sun out, the air was icy, particularly as the wind grew stronger.

Back in the woods, under the thickest trees, we found some dry wood. Tiffany couldn't carry much because of her bad ankle and crutch, but she helped. After a couple of hours, we had a big pile of different sizes of wood pieces. I built a small tepee of twigs, and we were ready to light the fire.

"I'm afraid this wind will put out our flame," I said. By now it was whistling through the trees and whooshing across the meadow. Getting a fire going was delicate work. I didn't want to succeed only to have the wind blow it out.

"We could build a snow wall to protect the flame from the wind," Tiffany suggested.

"Good idea."

So we worked for another hour and a half, building the wall. Once Mom, Dad, and I had built an igloo for fun. I decided to build the wall like we had built our igloo. I made snowballs and rolled them across the meadow. When they were nice and big, I pushed them up to our camp. Soon we had a semicircle of snowballs around the twig tepee and wood pile. Then I rolled smaller snowballs and set them on top of the big ones. Tiffany helped by packing snow in the holes and cracks between the snowballs.

By the time we were finished, we had a partial igloo. It stood about four feet high and was shaped like a big C around our camp.

"Where are we going to sit?" Tiffany asked.

Amy used to tell me she would make her bed out of dried moss. I didn't see any moss, but we could use pine and cedar branches. They wouldn't be as soft, but they'd be a lot warmer than snow. So I cut more boughs and used them to cover the ground inside our half-built igloo.

We had spent the entire afternoon working. The sun was already low in the sky, and the wind struck my aching arms and legs like cold slaps. I was so tired, I could barely walk. My legs kept buckling beneath me.

"Let's light the fire," I said. "Want me to get the matches out of your knapsack?"

Tiffany was putting some finishing touches on the wall, packing extra snow in the cracks. She turned and looked at me. Her jaw fell open, but she didn't speak for a long time. Then she said, "I thought *you* had matches."

"What? *You're* the one who said, 'Let's build a fire.' "

"*You're* the one who's lived in the Sierras your whole life. I figured you'd know enough to bring matches."

"We were only coming out here for a couple of hours, remember? Why would I have brought matches?"

I looked at our perfect little tepee of twigs. I looked at our big pile of wood. I looked at the strong snow fort surrounding our camp. We had been so smart . . . all for nothing.

"We could try . . . ," Tiffany said, picking up two pieces of dry wood. She vigorously started rubbing them together. I knew that wouldn't work. I'd tried it a million times and never gotten so much as a spark.

I sat down on the bed of evergreen branches, more exhausted than I'd ever felt in my life. Looking up, I saw three hawks circling in the late afternoon sky. I pretended they were tiny airplanes. Tiny rescue airplanes.

It would be getting dark soon. And much colder. Even if I wanted to return to the bobcat den, even if I could talk Tiffany into it, I didn't think we should. We should stay out in the open so that if there *were* any rescue planes, they would see us. I just hoped we wouldn't freeze to death during the night.

"I'm going to the bathroom," Tiffany said.

"First tree on your left," I said, trying for a joke.

The corners of her mouth lifted a tiny bit, almost a smile. She limped, still using her crutch, toward the woods, then stopped suddenly.

"Hey, Erin, look."

A fresh set of tracks. These were tiny tracks. Some little critter had skittered across the snow.

The tracks came from the forest but ended several yards out in the meadow.

"Where'd they go?" Tiffany asked. "They just stop. That's not possible."

I looked all around. Nothing. Little footprints, then pure, untouched snow.

I thought of the hawks and looked up. "You're not going to believe this," I said.

"What?"

"I bet it was a chipmunk. And I bet a hawk swooped down, grabbed it, and carried it off for supper."

The wind whipped Tiffany's hair into her face, but I could still see the fright.

"Hawks eat chipmunks," I said.

"Okay," Tiffany said, shaking herself. "Well, there's not much daylight. We'd better document these chipmunk tracks."

I couldn't believe it. Tiffany was still working on our science project! She hopped back to camp and got her knapsack. Returning, she handed me the camera. I was about to tell her to forget about the science project—we had to concentrate on saving our lives. But I liked the way she assumed we'd get through this, that we still had to do ordinary things, like turn in our science project. So I took pictures of where the chipmunk tracks ended, then of the hawks, though I doubted they were big enough to show up in the pictures. Tiffany measured and drew the tracks.

By the time we finished, the sun sat on the mountaintop to the west. We watched the bright orange ball quickly sink and disappear. Instantly the air felt much colder. I thought about how we'd be warmer in the bobcat den than out here. But bobcats were predators, after all. I didn't want to be bobcat prey.

We would have to spend the night in the open, under the stars. At least it wasn't snowing, and there would be that nice, big moon.

I put an arm around Tiffany so that she could lean on me as we made our way over to our little fort. Even if we didn't have a fire, the snow wall would block the wind and the bed of evergreen boughs would be better than lying on the snow.

"Wait," Tiffany said, pulling away from me. She cupped her ears.

"What?"

"Listen!"

Then I heard it: a dull roar. A moment later, I saw a small airplane.

The tiny plane, probably a four-seater, flew right over the mountaintop in the distance. It was headed for our meadow.

Everything inside me melted all at once. They had found us! I would sleep in my own warm bed tonight after all.

Tiffany started shouting, "Right here! Help! Right here!"

She waved her crutch in the air over her head. I jumped up and down, too, waving my arms like I was doing jumping jacks.

The airplane drew closer and closer. Soon it was directly overhead, right over our meadow. In a moment, it would circle and then land. We would climb on board. Then we would fly home to hot suppers and warm homes.

10: Pioneer Ghosts

TIFFANY AND I danced in the meadow, screaming and cheering, waiting for the plane to begin its descent.

It didn't. It kept right on going. It flew over the meadow and disappeared behind the mountains. The sound of its engine grew fainter and fainter.

"It's coming back, isn't it?" Tiffany asked.

"Maybe it's circling so that it can land better," I suggested.

But a moment later, we couldn't hear the plane at all. The pilot must not have not have seen us. It must have been too dark already.

"All right," Tiffany said. "I *know* there'll be another plane. We have to write 'SOS' in the snow."

"With what?"

"Tree branches."

"Good idea." I could have kicked myself for not having thought of it sooner. I sure had been wrong abut Tiffany—even though she grew up in the city, she had a lot of good ideas. "But let's wait until morning. It's nearly dark. No one could see it anyway."

Besides, I was so tired I could barely move.

The moon hadn't yet risen, but the stars began to pop to life in the clear sky. We wrapped ourselves in the space blanket and lay down on the branches inside our roofless igloo. I tried not to look at the unlit tepee of twigs.

I also tried not to think about the gnawing in my stomach, but it was hard to ignore. Every few minutes, my stomach snarled out loud.

"I'm cold," I said.

Tiffany was quiet for a minute, then she said, "See the stars?"

I grunted an answer.

"Let's pretend the stars are millions of campfires that people have built in heaven."

I looked up and pretended I could feel the warmth from all those campfires.

"It's true, you know. My brother says that stars are gigantic balls of fire. They are very, very hot."

"Too bad they're so far away," I started to say, but was interrupted by a long, piercing whine. It came from somewhere in the forest. A second later, a howl echoed across the meadow.

"Rescue dogs!" Tiffany cried, sitting up.

I wished she were right.

"No," I said. "Coyotes."

Tiffany stiffened.

"They're just wild dogs," I told her.

Then the coyote howled again. This time another answered, sounding as if it were calling from a different mountainside. Soon, the two packs of coyotes called back and forth to one another, a symphony of high-pitched barking.

The coyote concert was eerie. "They're nocturnal animals," I said, trying to make conversation so that Tiffany wouldn't be so scared.

"That means they hunt at night?" she asked.

"They won't hunt us," I tried to reassure her. Just then, one pack started up a particularly loud round of barking and howling.

"Okay," Tiffany said, cuddling up to me. "Pretend that we're twins. But our parents had a wicked enemy. He stole us the day we were born and put us in a basket and threw us in a river. We floated far downstream, then washed ashore. A mother coyote found us. So we were raised by a pack of coyotes."

I added, "We sleep in their dens and hunt with them."

"At night, they sing and we listen. That's what we're doing now."

Tiffany made up nice stories. As I listened to the mournful howling, I pretended that the coyotes were my family. Somehow, as cold and hungry as I was, I fell asleep listening to their songs.

When I woke up again, my whole body shook with cold. A bright light shined in my face. Where would a light be coming from? For a second I was frightened. Then I had a burst of hope.

Maybe the light was the bright headlamp of a snowmobile, coming to rescue us!

My lenses were completely iced over. When I cleared them, I saw that the bright light was only the nearly full moon. It sat over the mountains, on the rise, fat and glowing.

When the moon is full, it rises at the same time as the sun sets, so I must not have slept for long. The coyotes had quieted down, and now the wilderness was silent.

I looked out at the moonlit meadow, glad that the clear weather was holding.

Then I saw it.

Standing in the meadow, now more than twenty years away, was a large cat. It had a short tail with a black spot near the end and a white tip. A tiny pointed tuft of black fur stuck up from each ear. A big furry ruff surrounded its face. It was beautiful. I thought of Amy saying, "All living things are precious."

The bobcat stared back at me. I wasn't scared. Not at all. Now that we were face to face, I could tell that it wouldn't hurt us.

Suddenly the bobcat's ears pricked up, as if *it* were scared. The cat crouched down low, staring into the woods behind me. Then she leapt away, darting across the meadow in the moonlight. It was so bright, a shadow chased after her.

I wondered what had scared her so. Cats have much better night vision than people. What had she seen in the forest?

Somewhere back in there was the miner's cabin. I don't know why, but I thought of ghosts, miners' ghosts. It was possible that old grizzled pioneers still lived back in those woods. Their ghosts, that is, still looking for gold in the streams.

I forced myself to turn away from the forest, lie back down, and pull the space blanket over me. My feet were numb. At that moment I realized that we really might not get out alive. How long could we live without food or fire or shelter? Dad had said a *series* of storms. When was the next one due? Sure, the bobcat was beautiful, but it *was* a wild animal. What would it do to us if we tried to spend a *second* night in its den?

Worst of all, I realized that Officer Foster and Mrs. Jeffers had been right. My imagination had swept me away. I had come out here to rescue Amy, but, instead, Tiffany and I were going to die. My stupid capers, shenanigans, and escapades, as Dad called them.

Then I got mad. It was all Amy's fault. If she

had just come to say goodbye to me before moving to Tucson, none of this would have happened.

How long would we last? I wondered. Would we lose consciousness before dying?

My mind started to drift. As I began to nod off again, I half thought and half dreamt that I was a pioneer girl, crossing the Sierras a hundred and fifty years ago. My covered wagon had broken down. The rest of our party—including a man who looked like Officer Foster and a woman who looked like Mrs. Jeffers—wanted to leave me behind. They didn't believe I was tough enough to finish the journey, with or without a covered wagon. But some coyotes sang to me. And a bobcat guarded my camp. *You have the spirit of a wild animal.* I fell into a deep sleep.

A clomping, like heavy footsteps, awoke me. A moan, then a grunt, accompanied the clomping. The seconds drew closer.

A shadowy shape lurched toward our camp. The shape fell, groaned, heaved itself up. A moment later, a figure—a human figure—staggered into the moonlit meadow.

11: SOS!

KEEPING MY EYES on the ghost, I reached for Tiffany. She was missing!

I screamed, the sound tearing from the bottom of my belly.

A second later, the figure in the meadow screamed also, high and piercing.

I had terrified it . . . her.

Tiffany.

I made my way over to where she crouched, huddled in the snow.

"It's okay," I said. "Tiffany, it's just me."

"Why did you scream?"

"You scared me. I didn't realize it was you. What happened? Are you okay?"

She shook her head.

"What were you doing out here?"

"I had to pee. So I went a little ways away from our camp. I thought if I peed nearby, it might attract the animals. I'm so tired though. My crutch kept slipping. I kept landing too hard on my sore ankle."

"Okay, come on," I said. "Come back to camp." Then I realized that I had to pee, also. So I said, "I'll be right there."

I walked out into the meadow. She might have been right about urine attracting animals. I lifted my jacket and pulled down my pants. As I started to pee, something went *crunch*. The ground beneath my feet sank.

Water swirled around my ankles. The stream!

I tried to move, but the ice broke and I fell backward. The ice broke where my bare behind hit, too, and then I was sitting in the flowing water. The water wasn't very deep, maybe just a foot, but I was soaking wet from the waist down. I grasped at the ice with my mittens. If I tried crawling, I would just keep breaking the ice and falling in again.

"Here!" It was Tiffany, standing off to the side, holding out her crutch.

"Don't come any closer!" I called out. "I don't know where the stream edge is."

"Grab the end of my crutch!"

She held out the forked end and I grasped each side of it. I pulled myself up and stood in the icy water, my drenched pants still bunched around my ankles. Yanking them up, I tried to step out of the stream and onto the ice. It started to break, so I jumped forward. Finally, I was safe at Tiffany's side.

It was the middle of the night. I was soaking wet. And we had no fire. Even before we covered the few yards back to our camp, my jeans had begun to freeze.

"You have to take them off," Tiffany said. "They'll just make you colder now."

"I'll get hypothermia," I said, sitting down on our bed of greens.

"What's that?" Tiffany asked, helping me tug my wet boots and jeans off.

"It's when you become so cold, your body can no longer warm itself up. You get colder and colder, and then . . ." I didn't want to finish that thought. "My down parka is wet, too. Down feathers are useless when they're wet."

"Only the bottom part is wet. Keep it on. I have an idea about your pants."

Tiffany rubbed my feet. I could barely feel my toes. She wrapped my legs in her wool coat, then wrapped the space blanket around them.

"What about you? You'll freeze without your coat," I said.

"Just for a bit. Until I get your pants made. Give me your pocketknife."

Tiffany took out her wool dress, the one she had shoved in her knapsack two days before. Using my knife, she cut a slit down the front and one down the back. Then she made me pull the dress up like pants. Next, she cut the straps off our knapsacks. She used the straps to tie the dress around my legs, one strap at each thigh and one at each calf. Then we took the long cord out of the bottom hem of my parka and used that to hold the dress at my waist. My new "pants" felt a lot warmer than the night air.

"Now," Tiffany said, "We have to do something about your feet." She rubbed my toes again until they tingled

"My socks are wool," I said. "Wool stays warm even when it's wet. I'd better put them back on."

She took the wool hat off my head and pulled it over the wet wool socks on my feet. "There," she said.

I closed my eyes, suddenly very sleepy.

"Does that Girl Scout handbook say anything about hypothermia?" Tiffany asked.

"Umm." My mind drifted and my eye lids slid shut again.

Tiffany spread out the space blanket. We lay down, curled close together for warmth, and she pulled her wool coat over us.

"What about you?" I asked drowsily. "I have two coats now."

"I didn't fall in the stream. You're shaking really hard. Maybe you should try to sleep."

Suddenly the word "sleep" hit me like a slap in the face. I remembered everything now—the picture in one of my Girl Scout books of the girls in the snow and the caption beneath it that said you should learn the signs of hypothermia: shaking, drowsiness, and disorientation. If someone has hypothermia, you are supposed to put the victim in warm, dry clothes, give her warm liquids, and—above all—keep her awake.

"Tiffany!" I said trying to sit up.

She held me down, saying, "Stay under the coat."

"But I can't go to sleep. If you have hypothermia, you aren't supposed to sleep. You might not wake up."

I heard Tiffany's sharp intake of breath. "Okay," she said. "Don't worry. I won't let you sleep. But we have to stay lying down so we can warm up under the coat."

Not falling asleep was going to be impossible. I was more tired than I had ever been in my life. I thought maybe we should get up and walk to warm up and stay awake. But my boots were soaked, and, besides, I could barely move. All I wanted was sleep.

I shut my eyes.

Tiffany poked me. "Listen," she said, "and look at the stars." She described what our life would be like living as the twin human children of the coyotes, and I listened. Each time my eyes closed, she poked me in the side again. At times I thought I was dreaming.

Once I felt someone take the socks and hat off my feet and rub my toes. I felt the pads and claws of a coyote mother. The coyote shook my leg hard, then, and I came to. Tiffany was rubbing my feet.

She talked and talked to keep me awake. Her voice became scratchy and raw. I drifted, but she always made sure I stayed awake. The hours passed. The moon began sinking behind the mountains. The stars began to vanish.

The sun . . ., I thought hazily. When the sun came out, it would warm us. I knew that the sun gave energy to all life on earth. Usually I took that for granted. Now I gazed at the dark mountains in the east, where the sun would rise, and thought that I would never ever again take the sun for granted.

As daylight began to tickle the snow in the meadow, Tiffany took hold of my arms and hauled me up into a sitting position. "What we have to do," she said, "is make a composite drawing of Amy. That way, when we're rescued, we'll be ready to continue the search in a different way."

"I can't," I mumbled. "Too sleepy." My head felt like it was stuffed with feathers.

"Describe her," she insisted. She took the sketch pad and pencil out of her knapsack.

"She's real pretty."

"Erin!" Tiffany was annoyed. "That's not good

enough. You have to give me details. How long is her hair? What color? What's the shape of her nose? Are her lips thin or full?"

So, as the meadow lightened into day, Tiffany kept me awake by having me describe Amy's appearance. She drew pictures based on my descriptions, then showed me her sketches. I corrected them, saying things like, "Her eyebrows are fuller," or "her nose isn't so round." Tiffany erased and tried again. Finally she showed me a picture that looked amazingly like Amy.

"How'd you do that?" I asked her.

"You did it. You described what she looked like—from your *observations*." She giggled at her use of the science word. "And I *documented* your observations."

"If we get out of here, are you really going to help me find Amy?"

"Of course I am."

"What if she's just in Tucson with her mother?"

"She's not. She would have called you if she were going to Tucson with her mother."

I was quiet for a moment.

As f she read my mind, she said, "It's my experience that adults sometimes overlook the obvious. They're too busy to be good at observation. You're great at it."

"I am?"

"Sure. Come on. It's time to build the SOS sign."

"It's barely daylight." I didn't know if I could move.

"It's our only hope. We don't want to miss another chance. Who knows when the next plane will fly over? Besides," she said, "Moving will warm us up."

"I can't."

"Yes, you can." She stood up, wincing in pain when she stood on her bad ankle, and pulled my arms.

It took me a few tries to get up, but I finally did. I adjusted the knapsack straps on my legs so that the plaid wool covered as much skin as possible.

"Look." Tiffany pointed. "The sun is coming up. In a few minutes, it'll break over the mountains."

"My boots are frozen."

"Put them on anyway."

The growing daylight lifted my spirits a little bit and helped me feel more awake. I pulled on the rock-hard leather boots and tied the laces as best I could. Then I stood.

Walking was difficult. My muscles ached. Holding on to each other, we lurched into the woods to look for more branches for our sign. At least I could still feel my feet.

After going just a few yards, Tiffany moaned,

"My ankle. I think it's worse." She leaned on the crutch. Then she tried another step, her face screwing up in pain.

I thought: *Tiffany saved my life during the night. She made me pants from her dress. She kept me awake. Even while she was in all this pain.*

"Come on, I'll take you back to camp. Then I'll gather the branches."

"If you bring them to me," she said, "I'll lay them out in the meadow."

"Stay away from the stream," I warned. "Don't go very far out in the meadow."

"But we want our sign to be seen from the sky."

She was right. So together we probed gently into the meadow, looking carefully for the slight slope that indicated the stream bank.

When we found a place that seemed safe, Tiffany marked it by laying a branch from our fort in the spot. Then I told her to go rest in our almost igloo until I returned with branches.

Before going into the woods for the branches, I looked up, wondering why the sun hadn't broken out yet. It was clouding up again.

I forced myself to keep my mind on the task. We had to make an SOS sign. I had to get branches. I had to put one foot in front of the other.

Branches were hard to find. I had already cut

the ones that were nearby, on the edge of the forest, and low enough on the trees to reach. These were in the bed of our fort. I figured I could use the firewood for part of the sign, but it wouldn't be nearly enough.

To find more branches, I had to go deeper into the woods. I didn't like that idea much, but I had to do it.

My thoughts were like dreams. I couldn't focus at all. "Branches," I kept saying to myself. "Have to find branches."

I walked deeper and deeper into the woods, looking. All the branches were so high up. As I walked, I kept turning to make sure I could still see the opening of the meadow through the trees. I didn't want to get lost.

"Finally I found some low branches and began sawing them off with my pocketknife. I left them in a pile and walked forward a bit farther, where I found some more low branches.

That's when I saw, just a little bit ahead, a small clearing. The funniest-looking tree trunk sat in the middle of it. As I approached, I saw that it wasn't a tree trunk at all. It was an old rusted piece of machinery, round at the bottom with a big pipe coming out of the top.

An old potbellied stove.

The miner's cabin.

12: The Miner's Cabin

I APPROACHED SLOWLY, unsure of what I would find in the rotting remains of the tiny cabin. All four walls had caved in. A few decayed boards, covered with snow, lay on the ground. The big black and rusting potbellied stove was the only thing left standing.

At the sight, something in my heart also caved in. I'd expected Amy's cabin to be grand and magical. When she had talked about it, I had pictured warm smoke puffing out of a chimney. Fawns playing nearby. Maybe the smell of fresh bread baking.

Instead I saw ruins. Just ruins.

I poked around the old boards carefully, wondering if Amy really had been here in the summer. Maybe she made that up, too. Just like Justin hadn't really asked her to the prom, maybe he hadn't really shown her the cabin.

I was disgusted. I had come chasing after *this*— this pile of rotten boards and this rusty old stove.

Then I noticed something peculiar. There were tracks around the ruins. Human tracks. I estimated the size of the boot; about nine inches. And the waffle pattern of the tread was identical to the boot tracks we'd been following. But these tracks were fresh. They had to have been made since Saturday night.

Carefully, I circled the remains of the cabin. On the far side, I came upon a big pile of boards. They didn't seem to have fallen in that arrangement. Someone had piled them. They almost seemed to be a makeshift shelter. I knelt down and peeked under one of the top boards.

A groan, low and soft, came from within. My breath caught in my throat.

Slowly, I pulled off the top board so that I could see inside.

It was Amy.

She lay curled up in a wet sleeping bag. She wore no hat and her mass of black curls hung in her dirty face. Her lips were cracked and bleeding. A gash on her forehead was crusted with dried blood. I placed my fingers under her nose. I could feel her breath coming out softly. She was alive. I shook her gently.

She moaned again and flinched, but her eyes didn't open. Was she unconscious? Probably. She had been out here for four nights, with only these boards for shelter. Her wet sleeping bag wouldn't have kept her very warm; it was one of those old flannel kind. I carefully unzipped the bag. For clothes, she wore jeans, a sweater, and a fleece jacket. She clutched a knapsack to her chest.

I eased the knapsack away from her and looked at the contents. An empty Oreo cookies bag. A piece of plastic covered with the remains of something orange and greasy, probably cheese. An old bread bag. A book of poetry. And in the bottom of the knapsack, a book of matches.

Fire! I thought. *We can light our twig tepee!*

Quickly I opened the book of matches. It was empty. The matches were gone.

With or without fire, I had to get Amy back to our camp. We could keep her warmer there. I didn't know how much longer she would last. I thought *I* had been in bad shape, but at least I was conscious. I had to get the branches back, too, so that we could make the SOS sign.

Then a thought came to me. Amy had once had matches. She must have tried to build a fire. Maybe she had succeeded. Where would she have had the fire? Looking around, I saw only snow and soggy boards. The only possible place would be . . .

I picked my way through the old cabin junk to the potbellied stove. The door scraped on rusty hinges as it swung open.

Inside the stove were the charred remains of a

fire. I held my hand over the ashes. They weren't hot, but there was a bit of warmth.

Think hard, I told myself. It was difficult to keep my thoughts focused.

Think hard. I remembered how Dad and I used to build fires when we were camping. We would get a little flame going, then blow gently on the coals. He would remind me that it was important to blow from below, not from above.

I positioned my face so that my mouth was level with the bed of ashes in the stove. I blew very, very gently. A flurry of soot flew up in my face.

I coughed, then tried again, barely letting the breath out of my mouth. More soot.

Then again. This time I thought I saw a flicker of orange. *Please, please, please,* I thought. If I could get a fire going, I could warm up water for Amy. I blew again, and this time the flicker of orange glowed for a few moments.

Easy now, I told myself. *Slow and easy.* After a while, a charred piece of wood glowed like a coal. Then I needed kindling.

Of course there was kindling and lots of wood at Tiffany's and my camp. I could carry all that wood here, but that would be difficult.

Think hard.

I remembered reading about how the Indians used to keep their fires going. When they moved camps, they wrapped a hot coal in green leaves. They carried the hot coal to the next camp and used it to start the new fire. That's what I would have to do. After all, it was important that we stay in the open meadow, where we could be seen from the sky. And we already had a snow fort and a bed of greens there. Somehow I would have to get Amy and this hot coal back to camp.

I decided to transport the coal first. The fire was crucial. I tore some cedar branches from a nearby tree, making sure they were good and green. I used a stick to carefully scrape the hot coal onto a branch. Then I covered the coal with another green branch.

"Amy," I said, "I don't know if you can hear me. But I'll be back for you soon."

Finding my way back to camp was easy—I followed my own tracks in the fresh snow—but I was scared to death that the coal would go cold. I stopped every few yards to blow on it, very gently.

When I finally reached the meadow, Tiffany looked unhappy sitting by herself on our mat of greenery.

"Tiffany," I said, "I found Amy and a coal to light our fire."

A smile burst onto her face. She struggled to her feet and, hopping on one foot, came to hug me. I opened my mouth to warn her about the coal, but it was too late. Her foot caught in a branch and she fell, knocking me over.

"The coal!" I yelled as it hopped out of my hands. It landed near our pile of twigs.

"Oh no," Tiffany said, tears forming in her eyes for the first time.

I crawled to the coal and used a stick to nudge it over to the twig pile. "Maybe it's okay," I said. I leaned down and blow gently.

Again it took several tries before I got an orange glow, but I finally did. I rearranged the twig tepee so that it surrounded the coal, then kept blowing. The end of a twig caught fire.

A moment later, the tiny flame went out.

I glanced at the sky and groaned. The clouds were dark and swarming again. Even If I got a fire going, snow would put it out. Maybe I should have kept the coal in the potbellied stove. But it was too late to move the coal again. We had to start a fire.

"Some paper might help," I said. "Could you give me some notebook paper?"

Tiffany handed me two pieces of paper and I crumpled them up in loose balls. I placed them under the twigs and next to the coal. The paper caught. A tiny flame glowed inside the twig tepee. I watched as two twigs caught, then a third.

Soon the whole tepee burned. I carefully laid

some of the smaller pieces of wood against the fire.

Tiffany and I didn't speak until those pieces caught. Then she whispered "Fire" so quietly it sounded like a prayer.

"How are we going to get Amy over here?" I asked.

"I don't know." She looked around. "If we could only build a sled."

"Whatever we do, we'd better do it fast. She's unconscious."

"How far away is she?"

"Not very far. We've been near her all this time. Maybe about five minutes into the woods." I added more wood to the fire, then said, "Maybe we can make a stretcher using the space blanket. We can fold the sides over two long sticks and carry her."

Tiffany looked at her bad ankle and made a face. She could never carry half the stretcher.

So I said, "Or I could just drag her on the space blanket."

We were both quiet a moment. It sounded hard, very hard.

"You'd better stay here and keep the fire going," I said.

"Are you sure you can bring her back on your own?"

I wasn't at all sure, but I nodded.

Before I left, I placed my full water bottle close to the fire, but not so close that it would melt. Warm liquids would be good for all of us.

The hardest part, once I got back to Amy, was getting her onto the space blanket. I didn't want to hurt her, but she wouldn't wake up and she was too heavy to lift. I had to grab her under the arms and drag her over the boards.

I put her sleeping bag on top of the space blanket. Then I put Amy inside it and zipped the bag back up. Grabbing some sleeping bag and space blanket in each hand, I started pulling, but she was dead weight.

I decided to ditch the sleeping bag. Being wet, it was very heavy. So I unzipped it and rolled Amy onto the snow. I pushed the sleeping bag off the space blanket. I could come back for it later. Maybe we could dry it in front of the fire. It would be useful. For now, I had to get Amy to the fire. Looking at her lying in the snow reminded me of the time, after dancing, that she had lain in the snow on purpose, squealing with laughter and kicking her feet. Now she was motionless. I rolled her back onto the space blanket. She was much easier to drag without the wet sleeping bag.

While hauling her, I kept a lookout for sticks or anything sharp on the snow. We couldn't afford to rip the space blanket. As long as the snow was smooth, dragging Amy wasn't too difficult. I was glad when she occasionally moaned, because at least I knew she was still alive.

When I emerged from the trees, the fire was blazing. It was the nicest sight I'd seen in two days.

Tiffany helped me roll Amy off the space blanket and onto our bed of cedar and pine branches. "Wrap her in my coat," she said, taking it off. "The fire will keep me warm for now. She needs it more than me." We wrapped Amy up in the coat and moved her as close to the fire as we dared. I took the wool hat off my head and put it on Amy's. Next, I pulled off her boots and rubbed her toes. Tiffany rubbed Amy's fingers. They were white, almost gray, but after a long hard rubbing, most of them began turning pink.

I tested the water temperature in the bottle by putting in a finger. It was warm. I tipped back Amy's head and dripped a bit into her mouth.

I wasn't thinking about my own hunger or cold anymore. I didn't even feel tired now. My only thought was keeping Amy alive. As we tried to warm her, I told Tiffany all about the miner's cabin and how I had found Amy. Tiffany and I both drank some warm water, too.

I stared at the fire for a while, not wanting to leave its heat. A few snowflakes fell into the flames. It was time to make the SOS sign.

"I'll go get the branches now," I said, not wanting to think about those snowflakes.

I began to head back into the woods but stopped when I saw movement on the edge of the meadow, not far from our camp.

At first there was only a flash of yellow, then a blur of gray. Two coyotes trotted into the meadow just as a long howl echoed off the mountains. The animals stopped in their tracks. One lifted its nose and answered.

Then the coyotes noticed us. The gray fur on their necks stiffened and stood on end. One opened its mouth and I could see its teeth, ivory-colored and sharp.

I thought of what Tiffany had said about wolves attacking lame members of herds. Neither Amy nor Tiffany would be able to run. Then I stared at the two coyotes with their long thin legs and bright yellow eyes.

"Just wild dogs," I whispered.

13: Who I Am

ONE OF THE coyotes yipped, sounding almost like a puppy, and then they both ran into the woods. They ran fast, as if *they* were the ones in danger.

I suddenly felt silly for having been afraid. They were just trying to live. They'd been beautiful, just as the bobcat had been. Their legs were long and thin, their coats thick and gray, their eyes bright and yellow. How many people got to see bobcats or coyotes in their natural habitats?

All at once I was overwhelmed with a feeling of being me. It's hard to describe, but I realized I was a girl named Erin, a human being, who lived in this world of trees and other animals. I felt strong and happy—which is a funny way to feel when you're lost in the wilderness, starving, and very cold. I had been right all along about Amy, and Officer Foster and Mrs. Jeffers had been wrong. But now that didn't matter very much. What mattered was that I was alive. I felt a big swelling of love in my heart: for the bobcat, for the coyotes, for Tiffany and Amy, and for Mom and Dad.

That last thought prompted me to go get the branches. I loaded them up on the space blanket and dragged them as I had dragged Amy. While Tiffany tended the fire and Amy, I laid out a huge SOS sign. Then I joined them at the fire. Tiffany had arranged my wet jeans near the flames to dry them.

"Did you see those coyotes?" she asked.

I nodded. "They won't hurt us."

She didn't look so sure. "I thought you said they were nocturnal."

"I guess they come out in the daylight sometimes. It's still early in the morning. Maybe they're just getting in from the night."

"Where do they live?"

"Hey," I said. "I think she's waking up."

Amy's eyelids fluttered. "Who is . . . ?" she said.

I opened Amy's mouth and dripped in a bit more warm water. I wished we had something to give her to eat.

Her eyes opened. She looked right at me.

"It's me. Erin," I said.

"Erin? Where . . . ?"

"You're near the miner's cabin. Are you okay?"

"Miner's cabin . . . oh." Her eyes shut again.

"Amy!" I patted her face. "Stay awake, Amy."

She tried to talk, but her speech was too jumbled to understand.

I shook her shoulders gently. "You have to stay awake."

"I'm awake," she muttered. "Why are you here?"

That was a long story. I'd get to it later.

I asked, "Are you warm?"

"Yes, for the first time."

The fire did feel awesome. My own feet, hands, and everything were warming up.

"Can you tell us what happened?"

"I—Oh, Erin . . ."

"Help her," Tiffany said. "We know some of the story."

"Who's that?" Amy asked.

"This is my friend, Tiff—"

"Hoa," she interrupted. "My name is Hoa Tran."

I stared at her in surprise. I was about to ask, "What happened to 'Tiffany'?" Then I thought I understood. It was as if we both had been stripped down to our bare selves. I felt more like me than I had ever felt in my life, and maybe Tiffany—Hoa—felt the same way.

She helped Amy begin her story by saying, "So you came out here Thursday afternoon, right?"

"How do you know that?" Amy's words were slurred, but I could understand her.

"We know that," I said, "because you were in school on Thursday, but you didn't come to baby-sit on Thursday night."

"Oh, Erin, I'm so sorry."

"What happened then?"

"Mama went to Tucson Thursday morning. I told her I had plans with a friend and begged her to let me stay through the weekend. She finally said I could. I was supposed to fly to Tucson on Monday morning."

"It's Monday morning now," Hoa told her.

Amy went on, still slurring, "I told Mama I was staying with my friend and her father would drive me to the airport. Only I made all that up. Instead, I came out here. I didn't want to move to Tucson. I'm so tired of moving."

"I know how that feels," Hoa said. "I'm new in town, too."

"The first two nights were okay. I was cold, but dry. I read my poetry book. I looked at the stars. But then I realized I couldn't really live out here. I was going to go out on Saturday, but I didn't leave soon enough. It stormed Saturday afternoon and most of the night."

"We know," Hoa said. "That's why we're stuck out here, too."

"We had a shelter," I explained. "We stayed in a bobcat den."

"You did?" There was a tiny glint in Amy's eyes.

"Yes. You were in it, too. We know because your tracks went in one side and out the other. Remember the big tree with the branches that reach to the ground?"

Amy nodded. "I rested there on Thursday. But I went on to find the cabin."

"There is no cabin," I said, but I don't know if Amy heard me. She continued with her story.

"I tried to make a shelter, but it wasn't a very good one. I got soaked. On Sunday morning I got up and made a fire in the stove. But I had to stand, next to the stove, to get its warmth, and I was just too tired. So I got back in my sleeping bag, even though it was wet, in the little shelter. I got up a few times to feed the fire, but then I fell asleep."

"You were more than asleep," I told her. "You were unconscious."

"If Erin hadn't found you," Hoa informed, "you wouldn't have lived much longer."

"I was so stupid," she said.

"That's true," I answered. There was something else I wanted to know. "Amy? How come you said there was a cabin?"

"There *was* a cabin. I didn't know it was in ruins."

"Didn't you say Justin showed it to you last summer?"

Amy didn't answer for a minute. Then she said, "He didn't exactly show it to me. I heard kids talking about it at school. They have parties out here in the summer. They said it was a couple of miles from the highway intersection, just beyond a meadow. I thought they meant a standing cabin, something I could live in."

I felt another wave of sadness. Amy's cabin didn't exist at all. In a way, the Amy I thought I knew didn't really exist, either. She was just a scared girl.

I tucked the wool coat around her shoulders and pulled my hat more tightly over her head.

"It's starting to snow again," I said. "If it snows hard, it may put out our fire. We'll need shelter and—"

"Wait!" Hoa said, throwing a hand across my chest. "Listen."

In the next second, a loud hammering filled my ears. A helicopter swept over the mountain. Like a giant insect, it zipped toward the meadow. I knew I should jump up and scream and wave again. I couldn't move, though. I could only sit perfectly still, my heart full of hope.

The chopper hovered, then began lowering. I watched the long skis beneath the helicopter touch the meadow snow.

A man and woman jumped out of the chopper. They wore heavy, bright orange jackets, and they carried big canvas bags. They ran toward us.

Everything seemed like it was a dream, like it was happening in slow motion.

The medics wrapped us in warm blankets. They checked all our vital signs, like heartbeat and temperature. The man examined Hoa's ankle and shouted, to be heard above the chopper, to his coworker, "Twisted ankle!" He picked Hoa up and began carrying her to the helicopter. I noticed that she didn't let go of her crutch; she was taking it home. The woman picked up Army and followed him.

I don't know what came over me then. Some burst of feeling like being me again, I guess, mixed in with wanting to give Hoa a gift. So while the medics loaded her and Amy into the chopper, I reached for Hoa's knapsack. I found the camera. Then I ran, away from the chopper, over to the edge of the meadow where the coyotes had been. One of the knapsack straps came undone and my plaid wool pants flapped around on my bare leg.

Knowing I had only a few moments, I began snapping pictures of the coyote tracks. *After all,* I'd tell Hoa, *we still have to turn in our science project.* Someone swept me up from behind. I held on tightly to the camera so that I wouldn't drop it. The man ran to the chopper, carrying me. I had gotten two good shots of the coyote tracks. In my head I counted: human, rabbit, deer, bobcat, chipmunk, and coyote—six. We'd get a blue ribbon for sure.

As the man lifted me into the helicopter, I saw the other medic shoveling snow on our fire. She grabbed our knapsacks, two of which were strapless now of course, and ran to climb in with us.

The medics buckled our set belts, and the pilot spoke into his radio. "Come in, headquarters. Three youngsters found. All safe."

There was a scratchy sound over the radio and I heard a voice say, *"Three youngsters?"*

"Yes, *three*," the pilot said, and I couldn't help smiling to myself. Yes, three. Since no one had expected Amy in Tucson until this morning, she wasn't even reported missing yet. By anyone but me, that is. Soon, Mom and Dad, Officer Foster, and Mrs. Jeffers would all learn that I had been right about Amy's being out here and in danger.

The pilot continued, "We'll be back in fifteen minutes. Over and out."

Then he turned and told us, "Your parents are waiting at the ranger station."

We sat very still and quiet, wrapped in the blankets. The medics gave us sips of sweet hot chocolate from a thermos. I had never tasted anything more delicious. Then the chopper lifted slowly out of the meadow.

"It's all my fault," Amy said, as tears flowed down her face. "I'm sorry I got you into this mess. I was so stupid."

"That's true," I told her again. I thought of the miner's cabin that wasn't really there. I thought of all of Amy's stories, how she lied to me and to her mother. I felt sad for her. "We all could have died. But you know what? You weren't wrong about everything. A lot of what you told me was true. We made friends with a bobcat and some coyotes. A tree *did* hold us. And the birds *did* make our music."

Besides, I also had a new *human* friend. I glanced at Hoa and was surprised to see her grinning, her dimples deep and cheerful. I elbowed her and asked, "Aren't you afraid of how much trouble we're going to be in?"

"How much trouble can we be in when we've just saved someone's life?"

She had a point. I grinned back.

Hoa raised her hand for a high five. "For Girl Scout dropouts, we're pretty smart."

I slapped her hand, thinking about my surprise for her, the coyote track pictures.

Then I looked out the window as we zipped over the trees. In a moment, I'd see Mom and Dad. Soon I'd have a hot meal, a warm bed, and hugs from Snowball, Dorothy, and Scoot and Ooze and fish kisses from Lips and Fins.

The helicopter began to descend. I could see the ranger station parking lot below. There was a small crowd gathered. I held Amy's hand on one side of me and Hoa's on the other.

The chopper touched down on the parking lot cement. We had to sit still until the pilot allowed the door to be opened. Finally he did. Still holding hands, Hoa, Amy, and I climbed out and walked toward the crowd.

My glasses fogged right up, so I took them off. In the blur I imagined that all the people rushing to greet us were forest creatures, and for a moment, I wished that they were. Soon, I promised myself, I would return to the meadow for a visit.